BOOKS BY KATE BOLD

ALEXA CHASE SUSPENSE THRILLER
THE KILLING GAME (Book #1)
THE KILLING TIDE (Book #2)
THE KILLING HOUR (Book #3)
THE KILLING POINT (Book #4)
THE KILLING FOG (Book #5)
THE KILLING PLACE (Book #6)

ASHLEY HOPE SUSPENSE THRILLER
LET ME GO (Book #1)
LET ME OUT (Book #2)
LET ME LIVE (Book #3)

CHAPTER ONE

A ranch house in the Sonora Desert, five miles east of Benson, Arizona
July 3, 11 p.m.

Judge Antonio Rodriguez sat in his armchair going through some paperwork as a sports channel chattered in the background. It was a Saturday night and he shouldn't have been working, but a judge could never catch up on all the paperwork the job buried him in.

At the moment he was prepping for a murder case. Even though it wasn't due in his court for another week, he still had a mountain of paperwork to get through. Defense statements. Police records. The prosecution's statements. The evidence. It seemed endless. In a way it was endless, because he had six minor cases to get through before then, all with their associated piles of paperwork, and the work after the murder trial was beginning to pile up too.

While the regular, run of the mill criminal element such as drunk drivers and shoplifters gave him enough paperwork, it took a library to try a murder case.

The phone on the side table buzzed. He picked it up. A message from Carmen, his wife. He opened it and laughed.

A photo showed Carmen and her friends on the deck of a cruise ship, wearing sun dresses and straw hats and raising glasses of some colorful, fruity cocktail. A brilliant blue ocean shone in the background.

Judge Rodriguez ran his thumb lovingly over the image of the smiling woman, still bright and pretty despite her 62 years. Marrying her and sitting on the bench had been the two smartest things he had ever done.

He texted her back. "Looks like your traditional Fourth of July cruise is going well. Don't get pecked by a parrot like last year."

A text came back almost immediately. "Enjoy the game with the boys tomorrow. And STOP WORKING! It must be eleven there."

Judge Rodriguez laughed again. After a lifetime together, she knew all his tricks.

He emojied back a blushing face. "Emojied" was the right word, wasn't it? He'd have to ask his kids, both recent graduates and living in Albuquerque where there were more opportunities. Benson was a small town. All the kids left when and if they got a chance. Still had its share of criminals, though.

Carmen was right. Enough work for the night. He set his papers aside and turned up the volume on the TV. It was about time for his favorite commentators to give their view on how tomorrow's game would shape up.

The doorbell rang.

"What the—?"

A visitor? At this hour? Maybe Larry down the way was having trouble getting his car started again. He'd had to jump start Larry's old banger three times in the past month. Or maybe Irene, a bit further along the lane, was having trouble with the baby's colic. The houses in this neighborhood were scattered wide, everyone having several acres of desert to enjoy, but people still knew one another and gave a helping hand.

Judge Rodriguez lifted his heavy frame out of the armchair and walked out of his living room, past photos of his family at various stages of their lives, and into the front hall, flicking on the light as he did.

"Coming!" he called out. The doorbell did not ring a second time.

He unlocked the door, because even in rural Arizona it was wise to lock one's door, and opened it.

No one stood outside. His porch light was on, a few moths circling around the light, but within its pool of radiance there was no other movement. The front yard, the gravel driveway, and the dimly visible desert beyond were all empty.

A chill ran through him. Quickly he shut the door and locked it. Something wasn't right. The kids in the area were all too small or too big for such pranks. Which meant an adult had done it.

Judge Rodriguez switched off the front hallway light and, from the dim illumination coming from the living room, moved to a bureau near the front door where he kept a snub-nosed .38.

Carmen hated him having a gun in the house. She was a big-city girl from Phoenix, and wasn't used to that aspect of country living.

He could grab the shotgun he used for coyotes, but that would be too cumbersome to use inside and was all the way across the house in his bedroom closet.

Gripping the gun, he slowly backed away from the door, his mind wavering between concern and dismissal. It could simply be a prank from some teenagers passing through, like the time some young punks had painted one of the saguaro cacti on the street to look like a penis. Or it could be something more serious.

He had put a lot of bad people away, after all.

It was probably nothing, he thought. Heck, it might have even been an electrical problem. This house had been built in the Sixties. It had its little problems with aging just like he did.

A creak came from the back of the house, the unmistakable sound of his back door opening.

He had forgotten to lock it.

Judge Rodriguez broke out in a cold sweat. What to do? His phone lay on the side table in the living room. That might as well be a million miles away. He could move over there, but the intruder might hear him and he'd end up in the only lit portion of the house.

Better to stay here. From his vantage point he could see down the half-lit hall and into the kitchen. Since there was no light on in there and a light shining between him and that room, he couldn't see much of it. He couldn't see anything at all beyond. The little hall to the rear bathroom and back room, where the back door was, was out of sight around the corner.

Judge Rodriguez's ears strained to hear any sound of movement. He had become a bit hard of hearing in recent years, probably from thirty years of guilty criminals screaming at him in the courtroom, not to mention the heavy metal his younger son had been into in his teens and early twenties. So he didn't hear a thing, although that didn't mean there was nothing to hear.

Judge Rodriguez waited. A trickle of sweat ran down his brow. His heart pumped hard in his chest but the hand that gripped his pistol did not waver.

Still, no sound or movement came from the back of the house.

Had he imagined it all? He was tired and, as Carmen constantly told him, overworked. The doorbell might have been a prank, and then his imagination made up the sound of the back door opening.

Well, he wasn't going to wait here forever and hope the answer just came to him.

Slowly he began to creep down the hallway toward the kitchen. Every few steps he stopped, ears alert for any sound of movement. Still nothing. He was becoming more convinced that his mind had played tricks on him. A burglar would not target a house that had a light on, the TV making noise, and a car parked out front. A drug addict looking for something to steal so he could get his next fix would have made a heck of a noise.

And neither would have rung the doorbell.

Judge Rodriguez had ruled over a lot of cases of break-ins, and he couldn't recall a single one where the intruder had made himself known before breaking in.

So yes, this was probably all in his imagination.

He kept his finger on the trigger just in case.

Getting to the kitchen doorway, he popped his head around the corner, looking around its dim interior. No one. The short hallway leading to the rear bathroom and back room was almost black.

He stood there for a moment, peering into the dark and wishing he wasn't such a stickler for wasting electricity. Most people left more lights on.

Should he turn on the kitchen light? No, that would only alert the intruder, if there was an intruder. Judge Rodriguez had done a pretty good job of moving quietly. The intruder probably thought he was still in the living room watching TV.

Judge Rodriguez took a slow, silent breath, and began to creep across the kitchen, which smelled faintly of the frozen lasagna Carmen had left for him to heat up for tonight's dinner.

He got to the far doorway and paused. Still no sounds. Peering around the corner, he made out the dark outlines of the bathroom and the back-room doors, both open, on the left side of the hallway.

The back door opened onto the back room, which had little except a few potted plants and some boxes of old files. Nothing worth stealing. He did not feel a breeze coming from there, so the door was closed. Had the intruder gotten cold feet and left?

Most likely there wasn't an intruder at all.

He had to check, though.

Judge Rodriguez took a step into the hallway.

A flash to his left. A dark bulk rushing out of the bathroom. The brief, faint glint of light on metal.

Then a burning pain in his wrist. The pistol dropped to the floor.

Judge Rodriguez cried out, backing up into the kitchen.

The dark figure followed, making another swipe with the knife.

Just barely managing to raise his arm in time to protect his face, Judge Rodriguez felt another streak of hot pain on his forearm. He cried out, turned and ran for the hallway, hoping to get to the front door and out into the street where he could shout for help.

He barely made it two yards.

Another slash across his back. He gasped, staggered, and kept going, making it halfway down the hallway, just opposite the lit living room before another, deeper slash made him fall on his face.

He rolled over. The figure loomed over him, coming into the light from the living room.

Judge Rodriguez froze. He recognized that face.

In an instant he remembered everything about that case, and knew he could not hope for mercy.

The knife flashed down, stabbing.

The knife came up, trailing blood, and came down again.

And again.

And again.

Within two minutes, Judge Antonio Rodriguez of Benson, Arizona, lay wide-eyed in a pool of his own blood, staring at the ceiling as the world faded around him.

The last thing he heard after the back door slammed shut was his phone buzzing in the living room.

He would never see the photo of his wife blowing him a goodnight kiss.

CHAPTER TWO

East Jersey State Prison, Woodbridge Township, New Jersey
July 4, 10 a.m.

Deputy Marshal Alexa Chase waited as a prison guard buzzed her through a door of heavy steel bars. Her uniform clung to her as sweat oozed out of every pore in her body. The concrete hallway was cool, but Alexa could not stop sweating.

As the door clicked open, she and a second security guard entered a short hallway ending in an identical door.

The first door clicked shut behind them. The prison guard accompanying her adjusted his belt, heavy with a pistol, baton, and pepper spray, and nodded to his colleague through the security camera. The second door clicked open. Alexa surreptitiously wiped her sweating palms on the side of her uniform slacks.

Beyond lay a hall with six cells on each side. All were full. A red plastic chair stood in front of one at the end, positioned precisely in the middle of the hall so as to be out of reach of both cells. The prison guard and Alexa walked down the center of the hall as well. Alexa glanced to the right and left, keeping a wary eye on the inmates.

They kept a wary eye on her, burly, tattooed men sitting on their bunks or pacing back and forth in their tiny cells. Silent, Watchful.

East Jersey State Prison was a maximum security prison, holding some of the most violent criminals in the state. And she had flown all the way from Phoenix to see this ward's most violent offender.

Bruce Thornton, otherwise known as the Jersey Devil.

Several years ago, back when she had been Special Agent Alexa Chase of the FBI, she had arrested Thornton after he had made a string of killings in the Pine Barrens of New Jersey. It had been her toughest case yet—no pattern to the killings except the same general location. The victim were men, women, and children of all ages and races. Most had been kidnapped elsewhere and taken to the large forest area, except for one unlucky hiker and another unlucky hunter who had already been there. Some had been stabbed. Others had been shot or strangled. One ten-year-old girl had been buried alive.

She could see no pattern, no *modus operandi*, other than the obvious psychological importance of the location itself. Because beyond being a dense pine forest where it was easy to hide a body, it was the location of the famed Jersey Devil, a legendary creature with leathery wings, a goat-like head, taloned hands, cloven hooves, and a forked tail.

The media, of course, had already picked up on this and dubbed the killer the Jersey Devil. At first, local police had dismissed the connection, thinking the killer was merely using the barrens because it was so vast and easy to hide in. Plenty of other criminals had done so before, after all. Alexa thought differently.

She delved into the lore of the Jersey Devil—where it had been spotted, how it swooped down on its victims, competing theories as to its origin. The fact that it didn't exist didn't matter. It was the legend that was important.

Because she got the sense that the killer was trying to create his own legend.

Her research took her down a dozen rabbit holes, from folklore to Satanism, ecology to psychedelics, history to cryptzoology. It had been a disturbing, absorbing ride.

But it gave her the pattern of how he distributed the bodies, and it made her anticipate where his next kidnap victim would be taken to be finished off.

Two days of camping in the cold, rainy pine forest was rewarded with the appearance of Bruce Thornton, a terrified eleven-year-old boy in tow. When she leapt out of her hiding place, Thornton surrendered, a smile on his face and a triumphant gleam in his eyes. His legend had already been made.

Alexa had seen that gleam and almost killed him. She had raised her gun, aimed right for his head, and started to squeeze the trigger.

Bruce Thornton's smile had only widened.

And she had stopped, arresting him instead.

It was the biggest regret of her life.

She had wanted to kill him. No, she had *needed* to kill him. Some terrible, animalistic urge inside her wanted to hunt down this predator and show him that he was merely prey.

Just a couple of weeks ago she had nearly given in to temptation a second time, with a serial killer named Drake Logan. She regretted not killing him too.

So she had come here, to face the devil of her past.

The hallway seemed to extend in length, the red plastic chair pulling away from her as she walked and walked seemingly forever down a hallway that couldn't have measured more than fifty yards.

A low whistle came from the furthest cell, an off-key tuneless succession of notes. It took a moment for Alexa to recognize it.

Bruce Springsteen's "Night with the Jersey Devil." Bruce Thornton's favorite song.

"Whistles that damn tune all the goddam time," the prison guard muttered beside her. "You'd think with all this practice he'd get in tune."

Alexa squared her shoulders and walked the final few steps to bring her in front of the cell.

Bruce Thornton was nothing much to look at. Serial killers rarely were. Sitting on his bed at the back of his cell in prison orange and slippers, he looked very much like the out-of-work plumber he had been when Alexa caught him.

Only standing five-eight, with thinning blonde hair over a large forehead, beady blue eyes that never rested, a cheesy moustache that he never trimmed properly, and a squat body that ten years of prison food had added several pounds to, he was not an inspiring image for someone who wanted to launch a legend.

And yet he had. Countless books had been written about him. Several websites dedicated to his crimes. At least five documentaries.

No one had ever written a book about her. She was only a footnote in those books and websites, and she had turned down any interviews for the documentaries. She didn't trust the motivations of the producers.

No, the real heroes in those people's minds were the predators locked up in here. Disgusting.

"Hello, Special Agent Chase," he said, giving her a grin and showing off uneven teeth stained yellow from smoking. "I'd get up and shake your hand but Roy here would mace me."

"Damn right I would," Roy the prison guard said. He turned to Alexa. "I'll be right down the hall."

He moved off. Alexa sat in the red plastic chair, which was so flimsy it gave a little under her weight. No using this for a weapon.

"She's a cutie," a voice said behind her.

Thornton frowned. "Quiet, Rick."

Alexa turned around and saw a large Anglo man lazing on his bunk, his hand resting on his crotch. Deep acne scars pockmarked his face. He gave her a gap-toothed grin, but his eyes didn't smile. Not at all.

"My bad, Bruce. I'll just sit here and fantasize."

Alexa turned back to Thornton. She would have preferred a private conference with the serial killer, but to do that would have required the cover of an official visit, something she didn't want in the U.S. Marshals records. Thornton wasn't allowed in the visitors' room for security's sake, so she had to come to him. The warden stretched the rules for her, hoping she'd give him some insight on his most dangerous prisoner.

That was what Alexa was here for. Insight.

Thornton gave Alexa an apologetic shrug. "Rick's a bit of a ladies' man."

"Not in here he isn't," Alexa said, not bothering to turn around and look at Rick again.

The serial killer grinned. "Oh, but you should read his sheet. Before he got locked up, he had himself a time."

Rick chuckled.

Alexa glowered at Thornton. "Let's talk about you."

Another smile. "You mean us."

He gave a significant look around his cell. Alexa had been so focused on the man she had arrested all those years ago that she hadn't noticed the interior of the cell was entirely covered in drawings.

Most were crude, drawn on prison-issue paper with charcoal and crayon. They showed various depictions of the Jersey Devil, or dark woodlands with demonic eyes floating in the clouds above. Others showed Bigfoot or the Loch Ness Monster, or strange spirits flitting through haunted houses or dark woods.

"You do these?"

"Most of them."

"Some are in a different style," Alexa noted, pointing to a few on the righthand wall which were mediocre portraits of Thornton himself.

"Fans. I get a lot of fan mail."

A bitter taste came to Alexa's mouth. There was a whole subculture of people who corresponded with serial killers in prison. They sent them letters, books, money for the commissary, even marriage proposals.

It was sick. Simply sick.

In fact, after arresting the Jersey Devil, the FBI had been flooded with hate mail. Most of it was whacko stuff about how she had stopped a great ritual that Thornton was doing to bring mankind to a higher level of consciousness. Others were direct threats on Alexa herself.

Those were followed up and the authors arrested.

She looked back at Thornton, the old regret coming back tenfold.

"You missed the masterpiece," he said, pointing.

On the opposite wall was a drawing in Thornton's crude style. Alexa blinked. It showed her, seen from below, standing tall and proud in a forest glen, stars framing her head, pointing an oversized gun down on the viewer.

While Thornton was very far from being an artist, he had obviously put some extra time into this particular drawing. The resemblance was pretty good, and there was a power to the image. She looked domineering, confident, almost taller than the surrounding pines.

"That's how I always remember you," Thornton said with a smile. "You looked so strong, like an avenging spirit. A banshee or a Valkyrie."

"More like an FBI agent who busted your ass."

With prisoners, it was best to nip any sexual harassment in the bud.

But Thornton didn't seem intent on that. He went on in an admiring tone, "You see how I drew you almost as tall as those pines? That's how you looked. Fifty feet tall. You busted me when I had the rest of the FBI, Forest Service, state troopers, and a dozen different local police departments running around in circles."

"They weren't paying attention to the folklore."

Thornton shook his head. "No they were not. They just dismissed the whole Jersey Devil connection as an invention of the press."

This was why Thornton had been so hard to catch, and why he was not found criminally insane. He had set out to create a name for himself by deliberately tying his crimes to a local legend about a monster living in the Pine Barrens of New Jersey. The locations and methods of killing varied, but Alexa had noticed a pattern in how they related to the old legends. She was only able to figure out that connection after immersing herself in all sorts of dark knowledge thought up by superstitious and warped minds. It had seriously affected her metal state.

Aiming down the barrel of her pistol at this guy, about to stab to death an abducted child, had affected it even more.

She had almost shot him. Not because he resisted arrest, or because he was an clear and present threat to the child—on the contrary, as soon as she made herself known he had dropped his knife and put his hands in the air—but because she had simply wanted to.

No, *needed* to. All that fame, all that attention, even approval. While she remained a faceless officer of the law, an object of suspicion for a large portion of the population. She wanted to wipe him out. Prove she was the stronger.

Of course, all law enforcement officials have fantasized about harming criminals they have arrested. That's just the dark side of human nature. But she had come far closer than anyone should, and only pulled back at the last instant because the child was watching.

She felt sure if the kid hadn't been there, she would have gone through with it.

And she had regretted not killing Thornton every day in all the years since. Regretted that she didn't prove herself stronger than him.

And that regret had made her doubt her morality, doubt her worthiness to wear a badge.

Thornton was staring at the picture.

"So proud," Rick whispered from the other cell. "I look at that picture all the time and think, 'I could take that pride away.'"

"You'll never touch a woman again," Alexa told him without bothering to look at him. "Think about that."

"You got no style, Rick," Thornton said, flushing. "You're nothing but a common convict."

"And you're not?" Alexa asked, raising an eyebrow.

Thornton cocked his head. "Why are you here? You never visited me before. Living over the old days? I see you're a deputy marshal now. Read about you in the papers too. Caught Drake Logan. Twice."

"I wanted to see how you were doing."

As soon as Alexa said it, she realized how lame that sounded, and how untrue. She was here not for him, but for herself. She needed to face down this man who had brought up the darkness in her, a darkness that had only grown stronger during the Drake Logan manhunt.

Thornton didn't look convinced either. He studied her a moment as Alexa shifted uncomfortably in her seat.

"Yeah, you looked like an avenging angel when you burst in on me and that kid. Man, I thought you'd kill me for sure. Never thought I'd ever see someone look that fierce again. I sure haven't in here. Oh sure, there are plenty of tough guys in here, plenty of fights and guys getting bent over, but that real anger, that real strength, I've only seen it so strong in you."

Alexa looked away. Coming here had been a mistake.

Bruce Thornton, who had achieved his dream of going down in history as the living manifestation of the Jersey Devil, chuckled.

"No, never thought I'd see someone like that again. But I did. On TV in the rec room one day not too long ago."

Crap. I know what's coming.

"You looked like a champ beating down that guy Drake sent at you. And that look in your eye! Wow. The same look you gave me in the Pine Barrens all those years ago. What a sight. You had the whole rec room staring with their jaws open. Some of the boys hate you, plenty of them took a police beating themselves, but even they had to admire you."

"I used acceptable force."

Thornton laughed. "Acceptable force for an avenging angel. Oh, you can't trick me, Alexa. The public may be on your side, and the media might be on your side. You're the heroine who caught the big, bad Drake Logan, but I know, and you know, that you were getting off on that beating."

"Bet her panties got wet," Rick said from the cell behind her.

Thornton glowered at him. "Rick, shut the hell up or something's gonna happen to you that you won't like one bit."

"You make it sound like she's your girlfriend," the rapist/murderer snorted.

"No, she's my idol. Right up there with Drake Logan as people to aspire to be like."

"Drake's the man," Rick admitted.

"He's nothing but a common killer," Alexa told him. "And now he's probably going to get lethal injection."

Thornton cocked his head and looked at her. "The news said you made the arrest. Is that true or was that just to make you look better after that video?"

"I made the arrest," Alexa said with pride.

"You and a bunch of other people," Thornton snorted. "Because if you were alone with him, after he killed your partner and all, I bet you'd have capped him just like you wanted to cap me."

Alexa looked him in the eye. "I was alone with him, and I didn't kill him. I subdued him, cuffed him, read him his rights, and took him into custody."

Thornton tut-tutted. "Aw, Alexa. Now you're in a spot. Now you got two regrets, me and him."

"My only regret is I didn't catch the two of you sooner. I'm glad to see you rotting in here, though."

Thornton laughed. "What doesn't kill me makes me stronger. Drake Logan said that. And it's true. Catching us only helped our reputations. That little chase you had with him all over the Southwest is going to make his writings even more popular."

"His writings are banned in every prison in the country," Alexa said.

Thornton shrugged. "So are drugs. So what? We all love Drake's works."

"No way you're hiding his essays in your cells, but just in case I'll have them searched."

"You won't find anything. We got a man in here who's got a photographic memory. Was an accountant. Brilliant guy. Embezzled millions. Never got caught for it but he thought his boss and his boss's wife suspected him, so he killed them both. Got caught for that. Turns out he was a better embezzler than murderer. Anyway, he had all of Drake's writings memorized even before he got locked up. He recites them to us. In exchange, he gets to take his showers in peace."

"I'll be sure to tell the warden about that."

"I changed the details. The warden won't find him."

Alexa stood. This had been a mistake.

"I'll leave you to your cell and your showers. I'm going to go out, breathe some fresh air, watch a sunset, and maybe have a nice, tall, cold beer." Alexa stretched. "Ah, freedom!"

Thornton only laughed and clapped his hands. "Well done! Stick the knife in. That's what you like to do, Alexa. That's who you are. Now go on out and find yourself another killer. Go on out and get yourself another regret. Hey, if you're lucky, you might even help make another legend!"

She still didn't have an answer to Thornton's question of what she thought she'd get out of this. She had just wanted to face her past. And then what? Somehow the darkness would magically disappear? Somehow she could put her past mistakes to rest? Find some peace?

Now she felt even worse than before.

Thornton's applause followed her, echoing down the cellblock as she left.

But she wasn't leaving, and the Jersey Devil wasn't staying. A bit of her would remain here, and a bit of him would always be with her.

Maybe she could bury that bitter truth in work. Marshal Hernandez said he had a big case for her when she got back tomorrow. Maybe cracking that would help. Maybe doing some good in the world would outweigh the bad she felt in herself.

Maybe.

CHAPTER THREE

U.S. Marshals Field Office, Phoenix, Arizona
The Next Day

Alexa had never felt better about going back to work after a vacation.

Meeting with the Jersey Devil hadn't given her the inner peace and closure she had hoped for, but it sure did fire up her enthusiasm for capturing bad guys. People like Thornton needed to be behind bars, and there were plenty of people like Thornton who weren't.

Maybe she could fix that for a couple of thugs in the coming days. Her boss, Marshal Juan Hernandez, said he had a new assignment for the experimental collaboration between the U.S. Marshals Service and the Federal Bureau of Investigation. After flying back from the East Coast the previous night, Alexa caught some sleep and was up bright and early to get into Phoenix to hear what the next fight would be.

The public might imagine the Phoenix office of the U.S. Marshals Service to be in some old adobe home, or a dusty wooden building at the edge of the desert, a few gun-slinging cowboys leaning back in their chairs with their feet up on the railing, smoking hand-rolled cigarettes and looking out across the desert from under the brim of their ten-gallon hats.

That might have been how Marshals were a hundred years ago, but now the Phoenix office was housed at 111 West Monroe St., a glass and steel high rise in the middle of the Southwest's biggest city. The Marshals shared the building with several high tech companies, law firms, and financial advisors. There was an expensive bar on the ground floor Alexa had never been to. Her uniform would have looked out of place among all those suits and would have probably ruined the party.

At least she kept the ten-gallon hat. The best thing for the Arizona sun. Those high-paid suits could get skin cancer if they wanted to. She would dress for the climate.

Alexa walked through the front entrance of the building in full uniform—blue slacks, blue shirt with "Deputy US Marshal" emblazoned in white across the back, a Glock automatic pistol in the holster at her belt, and the six pointed star badge that her mentor, the late Robert Powers, had pinned on himself at her induction ceremony. The cool tile in the lobby clacked under the steps of her cowboy boots.

The security guard at the front desk asked for her ID and then waved her through. All the front desk people knew her, but the security company here ran a tight ship and you had to show ID no matter what, especially if the metal detector screamed a warning about your gun, your extendable baton, your large can of pepper spray, and your handcuffs.

She spotted her temporary partner from the FBI, Special Agent Stuart Barrett, sitting in one of the cushy chairs in the lobby, flipping through a car magazine. Wearing the standard federal suit, he looked much like many of the other business types passing through the lobby, except for the lack of a briefcase and the tell-tale bulge of a shoulder holster underneath his jacket. Stuart was a broad-shouldered, somewhat short man with close-cropped blonde hair, blue eyes, and a round, youthful face that made him look several years younger than his actual thirty-three.

Stuart put the magazine down and stood.

"Heard you come in," he joked, shaking her hand and gesturing toward the metal detector. "That thing is annoying."

"How have you been?" Alexa asked. She hadn't seen him for two weeks and it was good to see him again.

That surprised her a bit, because he had not made a good first impression. Bossy, arrogant, out of his depth in the West, and seemingly not the sharpest knife in the drawer. But he had hit the ground running in the Drake Logan case and while he still didn't know the difference between a barrel cactus and a tarantula, he had proved himself to be a shrewd thinker and a tough man in a fight.

Stuart gave her a smile. "I had to go back to Quantico and clean out my desk as well as ditch my apartment. Then I drove down here."

"You drove all the way across country?"

He brightened. "Yeah, it was great. Passed through the South and saw a bunch of Civil War battlefields, then across Texas and New Mexico. Damn, West Texas is boring."

"You don't like driving through several hundred miles of flatlands?"

"Ugh. I thought I'd never get across. Imagine doing it in the old days on horseback."

"Actually I did it a few years ago on horseback."

"You're certifiable. Let's go see your boss."

They took an elevator up. As the lights shone on each floor button one after another, Stuart asked, "So how was your vacation?"

"Spent the weekends on the family ranch riding. Took Stacy up."

"I bet she had a great time."

Stacy was a thirteen-year-old neighbor girl with alcoholic parents. Alexa spent more time taking care of her than they did.

"She loved every minute of it. My dad and brothers adore her, so she got doted on the entire time."

Stacy had basked in the attention; she didn't even mind doing her share of the work around the ranch. Now if only Alexa could get her to wash the dishes after she used them. And do her homework without having to hover over her every school night.

The elevator pinged and the door opened. They passed through a front office where a receptionist signed them in and sent them through to Marshal Hernandez's office.

While her boss's office had modern furnishings and looked out over Phoenix's downtown cluster of skyscrapers, Marshal Hernandez looked every inch the cowboy.

More accurately, a *vaquero*, the Hispanic cowboys who had ranged across this region before it was taken by the United States after it defeated Mexico in 1848.

Marshal Hernandez was a stocky Mexican-American with a thick moustache peppered with gray just like his close-cropped hair. Deep worry lines were permanently etched into his weathered face, but those lines seamed into a smile as he caught sight of Alexa.

"You're looking rested from your vacation, Deputy Marshal."

Appearances can be deceiving. I should have seen Thornton first, and then gone to the ranch later.

"I'm very rested, sir."

He shook her hand, then Special Agent Barrett's. "Good to see you as well, Special Agent. Are you two ready for a new assignment?"

"Yes, sir," they said together.

"Good. Sit. You have a big job ahead of you and you need to start right away."

Alexa felt the old familiar tingle. The lure of the hunt. Her dad and her brother Wayne liked to hunt javelina and coyotes out in the desert, but she had never gone along. She preferred to hunt wild animals that stood on two legs.

Marshal Hernandez rifled through some folders before handing them one. Alexa opened it while Stuart leaned in to look. Inside were two thin stacks of papers, each paperclipped together. Alexa grimaced. It was always a bad sign when you got a thin file at the beginning of a case. It meant there wasn't much evidence.

Flipping through the first stack, she saw a photo of an elderly Anglo man in judge's robes, followed by a brief bio of his career. Then came photos of a crime scene. The man had been stabbed to death in his own house. The second stack showed a Hispanic judge, also stabbed to death in his own house.

"Judges Mark Warburton and Antonio Rodriguez," Marshal Hernandez said. "Judge Warburton was killed in his house in Scottsdale on the night of June 30. Judge Rodriguez was murdered in his house near Benson on the night of July 3. In both cases the victims were stabbed to death. In both cases they were alone at home. Neither lived alone. Judge Warburton lived with his wife, who was out at a charity meeting at the time. She discovered the body when she came home. Judge Rodriguez also lived with his wife, but she was off on a cruise with friends. She's been notified and is returning home."

"So the killer waited to get them alone," Alexa murmured. "Didn't want witnesses and perhaps didn't want to have to kill someone besides the target."

"Might not care on the second count," Stuart said. "It might be just that it's easier."

Alexa nodded. "He also might have wanted to take his time, talk to his victim before killing him. Any signs of a struggle?"

"Not much," Marshal Hernandez said. "Warburton was in his seventies and frail. He was due to retire at the end of the year. Rodriguez wasn't in good shape either. Defensive wounds on the hands and arms. That's it."

"Physical evidence?" Alexa said, flipping through the CSI report and finding it depressingly scant.

"No fingerprints. Plenty of hair samples that they're running through DNA analysis."

Alexa made a face. There were always plenty of hair samples in a home case. That didn't mean any of them were the murderer's. And no fingerprints? No footprints or other evidence? This guy was good. Careful. And he played for high stakes. Killing a judge would guarantee you the death penalty in this state. This was going to be tough.

As she flipped through more of the crime scene description, she found that neither man had a camera system installed.

"I don't suppose the neighbors saw anything?" Stuart asked.

Marshal Hernandez shook his head. "There's not much to go on, but I want you two to take this. We were going to give you some organized crime cases to solve, but this takes priority. The killing of a judge puts it in the remit of the U.S. Marshals Service. The fact that there were two victims makes us worried that we're dealing with a serial killer. So this is a perfect case for the new FBI/Marshals collaboration. We're going on the theory that it was the same killer and it has something to do with an old case or cases these judges tried."

"Seems reasonable," Alexa said. "Where are the bodies?"

"Both are in the morgue here in Phoenix."

Alexa looked at Stuart. "We'll go check those out first. Then we'll go to the Scottsdale home."

"How far away is Benson?" Stuart asked.

This was the problem with the FBI man. While he was a lot smarter than he looked, and certainly brave in a fight, he was entirely unfamiliar with the Southwest. The last time they had to go through the desert, he was nearly bitten by a rattlesnake and spent several minutes pulling cactus thorns out of his legs.

"Two and a half hours. An hour and a half the way you drive."

Stuart grinned. "Then maybe we can get to that today."

"We'll see." She snapped the folder shut and turned to her boss. "Any other evidence? Any links between these two judges?"

"Not that we've found," Marshal Hernandez said. "I don't have to tell you this needs to get done as quickly as possible. The press hasn't caught wind of it yet, but that's only a matter of time, and not much time. Your job will get twice as hard once they're stirring things up. Sorry to throw you in the deep end right after your vacation."

"No problem at all, Marshal," she said, standing.

In fact, she preferred it this way. She needed to prove Bruce Thornton wrong.

And Drake Logan.

CHAPTER FOUR

Alexa led Stuart to one of her least favorite places in Phoenix—the coroner's office. It was housed in the basement of one of the larger city hospitals. They had called ahead, and the coroner was waiting for them when they arrived.

The coroner was a hunched, older man with wire-rimmed spectacles and a large bald spot. He resembled an academic and had a professor's quiet, authoritative air. After introductions, he led them into the storage room, where Alexa shivered from the cool air as they approached a line of oversized drawers. Names were written on tags for each of these. The two judges were side by side.

The coroner stopped and addressed them.

"Given your jobs, I am sure you have both been in a place like this. I must warn you, however, that this is an especially unpleasant sight."

Alexa and Stuart glanced at each other and then nodded to him.

The coroner opened up first one drawer, revealing a rather overweight Hispanic man, and then the other, which contained a rake-thin old Anglo man. Both were covered in slashes and punctures, now looking like red slits in their bloodless bodies.

The coroner was right. While Alexa had seen plenty of bodies, these two were especially bad. Both men had been butchered. Judge Warburton's right index and middle fingers had been almost severed as he vainly tried to protect himself from a vicious slash.

This is an attack of anger, Alexa thought. *The attacker slashed and stabbed at them over and over again. There are way more wounds here than necessary. And yet he maintained enough control not to leave behind any clues. Strange. I've never seen this before.*

The coroner allowed them a moment's study and then spoke. "Judge Warburton has 37 wounds and Judge Rodriguez has 41. Most are deep, showing strength. I would guess a male attacker although I would not rule out a strong female. This is an attack of fury, and poorly controlled. Only three of Judge Warburton's wounds would have been fatal on their own. None of Judge Rodriguez wounds fit into that category. From the angle of the wounds, several were made after the men lay prone. I suspect in the case of Antonio Rodriguez, the judge fell unconscious and was left for dead, quickly dying of blood loss."

Alexa nodded. She had guessed most of that herself, but it was good to have it confirmed by a specialist.

"Now there's something that was not in my preliminary report that you have already been given. I spent all my time in that report on the obvious wounds. This morning, just before you came, I looked more closely, and this is what I found."

He reached down and opened up Judge Warburton's mouth, an act that made Alexa crinkle her nose with displeasure. It seemed disrespectful.

She forgot her feelings when she saw what the coroner wanted to show her.

The judge's tongue had been slit down the middle.

The coroner moved around to Judge Rodriguez and opened his mouth to reveal the same thing.

"None of the tongue appears to be missing," Stuart said, his voice coming out a bit tight.

"No," the coroner confirmed. "No trophies were taken from either body. There was little blood in the mouth, which makes me believe that these wounds were done last, after all the other wounds were bleeding freely and little blood pressure remained to produce much bleeding from this wound."

"Forked tongue," Alexa murmured.

"The attacker must have hated them for some ruling they made," Stuart said.

Alexa nodded in agreement. "Hernandez has already given us access to their full court records. We'll start trawling through those right away. Do you have anything else to report, doctor?"

"Nothing at the moment. We're running toxicology reports."

"I doubt you'll find anything," Alexa said.

"I agree, but we must check. No traces of skin or fiber under the fingernails, unfortunately. Neither judge was able to grapple with the attacker. I'm afraid we just don't have much to go on. Oh, the attacker was right-handed, although the inaccuracy of the strikes might have been due not just to rage but to a left-handed individual trying to cover up by using his or her off hand."

Alexa took another look at the bodies, this time not focusing on the wounds, but on other aspects of these two judges. Warburton had the telltale impression in his right ear of a hearing aid.

"Was he wearing a hearing aid when he came in here?"

"No," the coroner said. "It doesn't appear in any of the crime scene photos either."

Alexa nodded. She hadn't noticed it on the floor near the body or anywhere else in the pictures.

There was little else to tell from Warburton. Thin, the slight inflammation in the joints from arthritis. Varicose veins on the legs. Otherwise, nothing of note.

Judge Rodriguez's body had even less to tell. Overweight. The faint scars of a hernia operation from many years before. No other visible ailments. Neither man had any visible STDs. That was something you always had to check in married victims—any hints that they had been playing around on the side.

But no. These looked like two solid, upstanding citizens, most likely killed because they were upholding the law.

What a waste, Alexa thought. *These guys devoted their lives to justice, and this is how they end up.*

She gave a little shudder as the image arose in her mind of her former partner, Robert Powers, getting decapitated right in front of her. He had died for justice too.

Briefly Alexa closed her eyes and got a hold of herself. When she opened them, she surveyed the human wreckage in front of her and sighed. No solid leads except the fact that both victims were Arizona judges. The key probably lay in their past.

But first she and Stuart needed to see the crime scenes and perform Alexa's least favorite part of the job.

Talking to the bereaved.

* * *

Francine Warburton looked like she had been a healthy, cheerful woman, active beyond her years.

No more.

Now Alexa saw a haggard old woman with no hope of happiness, trembling on the edge of her grave.

They met in the living room of a neighbor two doors down from the crime scene. The middle-aged couple had gone to the backyard as Alexa and Stuart sat in a pair of armchairs and the new widow sat alone on a long couch.

Wiping her eyes with a crumpled Kleenex, Francine Warburton asked in a hoarse, wavering voice, "I already explained everything to the police. Do I have to go through this again?"

"Just the basics, ma'am, and then we have a few other questions," Alexa said.

"Well, I was at First Methodist Church at the clothing committee. We collect clothing for the poor. We always go for coffee and pie afterwards so I didn't get back until about ten-thirty. I unlocked the front door and that … and that's …"

Francine started sobbing.

Alexa immediately took her off the list of suspects. Not because of the sobbing, which she had seen many a criminal fake, but because of the bodily reactions that were much harder to fake—the trembling, the dilated pupils, the ragged breathing.

She also looked too weak to have made the attack. While in the majority of cases where a married person is killed, it is the spouse or the spouse's lover who turns out to be the culprit; this woman was too old for a lover, too weak to have made those horrible wounds, and too much in shock to be a calculating murderer.

No, she was just another victim, almost as injured as her poor husband.

"Did you see or hear anything strange?" Alexa asked.

"No, except the door to the backyard was open."

"Is it usually locked?"

"The screen door is. On a warm night like that one, we usually leave the sliding glass door open to catch the breeze. Too much air conditioning is bad for my lungs."

"Do you have any dogs in your neighborhood? Were any barking?"

"No dogs that are close, except for the Chihuahua next door, and it's always kept inside. It never barks unless you go visit."

So no warning. And he might not have been wearing his hearing aid anyway.

"Do you have an alarm system?"

"Yes. We turn it on when we go to sleep."

"Do you drive your own car, Mrs. Warburton?"

"Yes."

So he might have been watching the house, waiting for her to leave. He caught Judge Rodriguez alone too.

"Are these meetings regular?"

"Every Wednesday night. I'm on the board so I attend all of them."

"Did you notice anything strange that night? Anyone you didn't know in the neighborhood? Suspicious vehicles?"

Francine Warburton shook her head. "The police asked me all of this. No, I didn't see anything."

That doesn't mean there wasn't anything to see. Most people are pretty unobservant. Especially when they're in the safe, familiar surroundings of their own neighborhood, heading for church.

"Had your husband received any threats? Had he been acting strangely?"

"No. I mean … he's had lots of people threaten him over the years when he's sentenced them. No one ever tried to hurt him, though."

"Did he mention any of those people specifically? Have any been released lately?"

Alexa didn't hold out much hope for this line of questioning. Stupid criminals threatened judges all the time. It earned them a contempt of court charge above and beyond whatever else they were there for. Some people were clueless.

"No," the widow said in a quiet voice before blowing her nose.

"Sorry for bothering you, Mrs. Warburton, and I'm terribly sorry for your loss. If you think of anything else, here's my card."

Francine nodded absently, her eyes looking into the far distance. Alexa and Stuart rose and left.

"Let's go check out the house;" she said, taking a big breath of fresh air as they got outside. She found herself regretting that the crime scene was so close. She could use a nice, long trek in the desert to clear her head.

As they walked the short distance to the Warburton home, they glanced around the neighborhood. The houses here were the typical affluent Arizona homes, rambling ranch structures with big gardens enclosed with five-foot wooden fences. Not too hard to hop over and providing full cover once you're inside. It never ceased to amaze Alexa how many people lived in a false sense of security.

Each house had a couple of acres of land, mostly given over to cultivated desert, a few ornamental cacti instead of the richer, more natural combination of cacti, scrub, and the occasional patch of dry, rustling desert grasses. The sun was at its height, and the temperature was nearing a hundred. Stuart looked like he was baking in his black suit. She'd have to get him to start wearing a hat at least.

The Warburton home was surrounded by police tape. They ducked under this, unlocked the door with a key provided by the police, and entered.

There was something about a house that had experienced a murder that always made it feel empty. The fully furnished rooms, the smells of cologne and yesterday's cooking, the family pictures on the walls, none of that could dispel Alexa's sensation that she was entering a giant, abandoned warehouse. She half expected their footsteps to echo.

The CSI team had come and gone. Now all that was left was a crimson bloodstain at the doorway between the hall and the master bedroom, and a chalk outline showing where one of the state's most experienced judges had breathed his last.

Stuart looked at a floorplan of the house from the file Marshal Hernandez had given them and pointed.

"Back door is this way."

They passed through to the back of the house, where a large kitchen and dining area gave access to the back yard through a sliding glass door and screen door. The pictures from the crime scene showed both doors open. They were now closed, leaving the kitchen hot and stuffy.

Alexa opened them. The screen door was already open an inch and she quickly saw the reason why. The little metal hook that secured the door to the doorframe was bent. The metal eye into which it went into the doorframe was also twisted.

"Doesn't take much strength to do that," Stuart said. "But with that little handle it probably left his fingers sore."

"I don't think the killer cared."

"Not the way he butchered the judge. He was focused on nothing but his mission."

"He or she," Alexa corrected. "We can't make assumptions at this stage."

"No, I guess not. But 99 percent chance it's a guy. The rage … "

Alexa nodded. He was probably right. Women rarely committed crimes of this sort of savagery. Not that women couldn't be savage, but they tended toward more subtle methods such as poisoning or hiring hitmen.

But this wasn't a hitman. Too much emotion involved. Could it be more than one person? They had no evidence for that but nothing could be discounted at this stage.

They headed out to the yard. A hummingbird fluttering at a feeder hanging from the branch of a mesquite tree sped away. Along one side of the fence, a carefully tended flowerbed burst with color. Alexa couldn't help but think about the water Francine was wasting to grow northern flowers in the middle of the desert. She set that thought aside as unworthy of a woman who had just lost her husband.

The fence was nearly six feet tall and made of treated wood. They could see nothing of the adjoining yards. Stuart, although rather short for a man, was still a few inches taller than Alexa so he went to each of the three sides, stood on tiptoe, and peeked over.

"Our murderer climbed over from the yard directly in the back," he said once he finished.

"Why do you think that?"

"The blinds are up in that house and I didn't see any furniture or pictures on the walls. I think it's vacant."

"Let's go check."

The winding streets of this development were such that they had to drive nearly half a mile to loop around and get to the house directly behind the Warburtons'. Alexa saw no one on the sidewalks. This was the kind of neighborhood where people drove everywhere. Like with many parts of Phoenix, there were no shops within easy walking distance. That would have meant fewer witnesses to see the killer.

As Stuart suspected, there was a realtor's sign on the front lawn. The Iraq War veteran was turning out to be a handy partner.

"Our perp knew his terrain," Stuart said.

"Rage and planning. A nasty combination."

"The perp has probably been building up their rage for a long time. I'm thinking he, or she, couldn't act on it because the judges put him inside. Cons have a long time to plan revenge. It's a favorite pastime in prison."

"Could be," Alexa replied. There were a thousand possibilities, but that was the most obvious one. And in policework, the obvious answer was usually the right one.

Not always, though.

"We should see if any perps got sentences from both judges," Stuart said. "We should probably check if they got sent inside by other judges too. Our killer might not be done."

Alexa nodded grimly. "I'll call the CSI team and have them check out this lot and the area in between, see if they find anything."

"It's only one," Stuart said, looking at his watch. "Shall we go down to Benson now?"

"Tomorrow," Alexa said. "I don't think we'll see much there and the widow isn't back until tomorrow morning. I think we should spend the rest of the day digging into Warburton's and Rodriguez's court records. And we need to dig quickly. Our killer might decide to strike again."

"I agree about the need for speed, but with both of these guys having more than thirty years on the bench each, we're in for a long, hard slog."

CHAPTER FIVE

And a long, hard slog it was, the kind of grind that always frustrated and exhausted Alexa. By nightfall, they had gone through hundreds of cases from both judges' most recent years of service, compiling a list of those who had been released, or those who had connection to organized crime or gangs who might be able to order a hit from prison.

That list was depressingly long, even when they made a priority list of individual who had been tried by both judges. The next step would be to try and narrow those two lists down. Some ex-cons would be living in halfway houses, unable to slip out after dark. Others had to wear locator bracelets. The rest they'd have to eliminate one by one with regular police investigation. At least Marshal Hernandez got the cooperation of the local police forces to do some of the legwork. That would help.

"Why is so much of police investigation such uninspiring grunt work?" Alexa said, rubbing her eyes. She was having trouble focusing and she had a headache.

"We'll get some more grunt workers again in the morning. They all went home two hours ago," Stuart said. When Alexa turned to him, she saw that he looked as tired as she felt.

"If I stopped a driver with eyes that red, I'd test for marijuana," Alexa told him.

"Same to you. Let's call it quits. Start fresh in the morning."

"We have more to do."

"And no staff to do it with. We're grinding. We've been going full tilt all day and now we're getting inefficient. We'll get more done if we quit now and come back in the morning."

"But we need to get this done."

"And we will," Stuart said, standing up and stretching. "The regular staff gets here at nine. Let's get here at eight."

"Seven."

"Seven-thirty?" Stuart said hopefully.

"Seven," Alexa said, staring at the mound of paperwork they still had to get through.

"I've had drill sergeants who were nicer than you. All right. Seven it is."

Alexa stood, wobbled a little at the sudden change of blood pressure, and realized she hadn't left the chair since lunch time.

Stretching and yawning, she followed Stuart to the parking lot and got in her truck.

She loved her job. It made her feel useful and on the side of right, but it sure could be flattening at times.

Which is why she didn't mind a long drive home at the end of the day.

She had deliberately chosen a house outside of Phoenix so she could enjoy living in the desert she loved when she wasn't at work. And she had picked a house to the west of town so she could enjoy Arizona's serene sunrises as she went to work, and its breathtaking sunsets as she returned home.

Arizona's big sky did not disappoint.

The sun was a boiling red disk on the horizon, turning the entire desert crimson. Up above, a few striated clouds were of the same color, in beautiful contrast to the sky's deepening blue. As Alexa left the last of the suburbs behind, she opened the window and breathed in the sweet smells of the desert, a mingling of creosote and mesquite, mixed with the sharp smell of hardpacked clay lightened by the faint, soft smell of vegetation. This was no Sahara. There was life here.

Taking U.S. Route 60, she passed through Morristown, a hamlet on its way to becoming a ghost town, and drove a mile on a cracked asphalt road, the car jerking a bit on the bumps, to her little ranch house. The porch light was on and Stacy's bicycle leaned against on the wire mesh fence. To her surprise, a car was parked out front.

Her heart skipped a beat. Someone was there with Stacy? She slowed the car, studying the situation. Then she recognized the light blue Lexus owned by Olivia Powers. Her police instincts made her read the license plate and confirm. She had a good head for license plates, and out of habit memorized all those of her friends and family.

She parked the car, her knee-jerk fear replaced by dread.

Olivia was Robert's widow. Besides a brief phone call, they hadn't spoken since Robert got killed. Alexa hadn't even been able to attend the funeral. She had been too busy tracking down the men who killed him.

But that was more than two weeks ago. Neither of them had called each other since. Alexa hadn't done so because she didn't know what to say, dreaded adding Olivia's grief to her own.

And Olivia hadn't called her because … well, Alexa didn't know. And she was terrified of finding out.

Did she blame Alexa for not stopping Drake and his team? Surely Marshal Hernandez had explained the particulars of the breakout, and how Alexa had been pinned and helpless in a crashed prisoner transport. But knowing and understanding were two very different things. And between understanding and forgiving stretched a vast territory of base emotion.

It would be very easy for Olivia, as kind and as loving a person as she was, to hate Alexa for what happened.

And Alexa would not be able to bear that hate.

She parked, wiped the sweat from her palms, and got out.

How long had she been here? And what was she saying to Stacy? Was she turning the girl against her? Telling her how Alexa wasn't the heroine Stacy looked up to, was a flawed and sometimes brutal woman who didn't deserve to wear a uniform?

The wall Alexa had carefully built between her professional life and her personal life might have already crumbled away, impossible to repair.

She hurried to the door and opened it. Olivia and Stacy sat on the couch, looking through a photo album. They both looked up when Alexa came in.

Stacy was a neighbor of hers, a petite thirteen-year-old girl in jeans and a Vans t-shirt, straight blonde hair reaching past her shoulders. She had a key to Alexa's house and stayed there whenever her parents passed out from drinking, which was at least three nights a week. What she thought of this strange woman coming to Alexa's house Alexa couldn't imagine.

Olivia stood, tears welling in her eyes. She opened her arms wide and they embraced.

All of Alexa's fears melted away. She had been wrong to worry what this kind, supportive woman would think. Robert had chosen to spend his life with her, after all, and his instincts were always good.

For a moment neither said anything, just sniffled and hugged each other closer. Alexa heard Stacy head to the kitchen. After a moment she could hear the girl preparing the kettle. Alexa always liked a cup of herbal tea after a stressful day, and Stacy was pretty good and detecting when those were. The moral support was definitely a two-way street.

Finally they let each other go and sat down. Oliva put a hand on hers.

"How are you feeling?" the widow asked.

You're asking me?

"Overwhelmed," she admitted. "Catching Drake Logan helped, but not enough."

"They'll be giving him the death penalty this time, I guess."

"Him and everyone involved in the prison bus break."

Olivia nodded. Her expression told Alexa she hadn't decided what she thought of that.

Sometimes I think she's too gentle of a soul to be married to an officer of the law, Robert once told Alexa.

"How are you?" Alexa asked.

"Sleeping better," Olivia murmured, looking at the floor. "They gave me pills for a while."

"I'm sorry I couldn't make it to the funeral."

"You were doing your duty, like Robert always did."

Alexa winced. She still wasn't used to hearing Robert referred to in the past tense.

Olivia nodded toward the kitchen. "Stacy's a wonderful girl. Robert told me all about her. Even though he never met her, he said you talked about her so much he felt like he knew her as well as anybody."

Alexa felt another tug of sadness. What Robert probably hadn't mentioned to Olivia was that Robert was the one who encouraged her to take Stacy under her wing. She had complained about how her neighbors in a nearby trailer had loud, drunken parties almost every night and their daughter would come to feed Alexa's horses without permission. The kid was feeding them everything from breakfast cereal to potato chips.

If you don't want your horses to get stomach cancer, Robert had told her, *Take that girl in, teach her how to feed an animal properly, and teach her how to ride. I never met a girl in my life who could resist horses.*

Alexa had taken his advice, and ended up with one of the most important relationships in her life. Yet another thing she owed that man. She couldn't even begin to count all the ways her life had been improved by him.

The clatter of something falling in the kitchen, followed by the sound of a breaking dish and several swear words, reminded her that this relationship wasn't always easy.

"Sorry!" Stacy called from the kitchen.

"She's a good kid," Alexa told Olivia. "Needs some guidance but I think she'll turn out fine."

"I thought you'd be home by now. Instead I found her. To pass the time I showed her a photo album of Robert's. I figured if he knew so much about her, she should know something about him."

She picked it up and handed it to Alexa. "He wanted you to have it."

Alexa blinked. "Me?"

Olivia nodded slowly. "He asked that you get a couple of things in case … "

A silence settled in the living room. To break it, Alexa opened the album.

The first page made the tears well up in her eyes again. It was a photo of her induction ceremony into the U.S. Marshals Service. Robert, an old family friend, had heard how burnt out Alexa had become after her time at the FBI, and how she had quit following the Jersey Devil case.

Alexa had fled back to the family ranch to stay with her father and brothers. After a period of time, she felt more rested, but also more restless. It was then that Robert Powers had paid her a visit and suggested she get back into her true calling—law enforcement.

She flipped through more of the album. The pictures were all of their career and time together. She remembered some of them being taken, like the one where they're posing next to a four by four loaded with cocaine. He and Alexa both held up plastic wrapped bricks of pure cocaine, each worth far more than they earned in a year. In another they were sitting at their favorite diner in Phoenix, and in another they were at a retirement barbeque for an older agent who had been a mentor to Powers.

Olivia managed a faint smile. "Robert was always a bit old fashioned. He never liked digital cameras or all those photo-sharing apps. I think he's managed to convert Stacy. She was talking about making a photo album too."

"Thank you. I'll treasure this," Alexa said, deeply moved.

"He also wanted you to have this."

Olivia handed her a leather-bound notebook. Alexa opened it and found it was full of pages in Robert's own tidy handwriting, with dates at the top of the pages.

"His diary?" Alexa asked. Why would he want her to have this?

"More of a professional journal. He said he kept his thoughts and impression of his work in there."

Alexa looked at her with surprise. "You never read it?"

"He asked me not to. He said there were things in there I … wouldn't like. You know how I always worried."

You were right to worry, Alexa thought, a lump rising in her throat.

Alexa looked back at the book. Why would he leave something to her that he asked his own wife not to read? What was in it? Professional advice? He had dispensed so much homespun wisdom and practical tips; Alexa couldn't imagine he could have had anything more to say.

"Thank you," Alexa replied.

Stacy entered carrying a tray. A teapot and three cups were precariously balanced on top. The sugar bowl had already spilled half its contents. How this girl could be so graceful on horseback and such a klutz in every other situation was something Alexa would really like to figure out sometime.

The tray made it to the coffee table with no further disasters and they drank in silence for a while. Stacy, who generally talked a mile a minute, seemed to sense the tense situation and kept quiet, staring at Olivia and Alexa in turn with big, questioning eyes.

The silence stretched out awkwardly. The more time everyone went without saying anything, the more uncomfortable Alexa felt. She desperately tried to think of something to say and couldn't come up with anything that didn't sound stupid.

She almost gasped with relief when Olivia spoke first.

"I'm awfully glad I got to meet little Stacy here. Robert says you have a good little sidekick and I see he's right."

Alexa winced as she heard Oliva refer to her husband in the present tense again. And that smile Olivia was making came out lopsided, as if it took a conscious effort.

It probably did.

"She takes good care of my horses when I'm away," Alexa said.

"She showed them to me. Lovely animals. A pity we never had any of our own."

Olivia's hand shook as she put the tea cup back on the saucer. The silence began to draw out again.

Olivia stood, a sudden movement that made both Alexa and Stacy jerk. If the widow noticed it, she didn't make any sign. "Well, I need to be going. Sorry I dropped in unannounced, but I can't bear the phone at the moment. Too impersonal."

"Not a problem at all. And if there's anything you need … "

Alexa had always thought saying that to a person who had just lost someone sounded agonizingly inadequate. What she needed was her husband.

But what else was there to say?

As Olivia pulled out of the drive, Alexa let out a breath of relief. No matter how good a woman Olivia was, no matter how understanding about Robert Powers's death, just seeing her made Alexa feel guilty.

She turned back to find Stacy sitting on the sofa looking over at the journal and photo album. She hadn't touched them. Stacy was always careful about rules until she knew what they were. When you live with raging alcoholics for parents, you don't know what normal is.

"Your partner left you his diary?" the teenager asked.

"Looks like," Alexa said, eyeing the leather-bound volume.

"I wonder what's in it."

"So do I."

"Are you going to read it now? I can watch TV or something."

"No. Tomorrow. I've got an early start. I need to go to Benson."

Stacy slumped a little. "Another case."

Alexa sighed. "Always another case."

"How long are you going to be gone?" The question came out as a whine.

Alexa put a hand on her shoulder. "I don't know. You know you're always welcome here." She jabbed a finger at her, trying to look stern. "But you know better than to let strangers into the house."

Stacy looked confused. "She's a woman."

"That doesn't matter. You know how many women I've arrested for violent crime?"

"Not as many as guys."

"That's not the point."

As soon as she said it, Alexa knew she had spoken with too much heat. Stacy's face didn't fall; it collapsed. The poor girl got no affection at home. No guidance. She came here to feel like she was welcome, and anything more than gentle chiding to wash the dishes or make her bed was greeted like Alexa was telling her she never wanted to see her again.

The girl slumped, staring at the floor and looking every bit as bereft as Olivia had a few minutes before.

Alexa sat down next to her and put an arm around her shoulders.

"Sorry for snapping at you. It's just I want to know you're safe. There are a lot of bad people in the world."

"Sorry. I'm dumb."

"You are not dumb." Some snooty girl in her class, who got straight As, had told Stacy she was dumb. Stacy was a C student. How could she be anything else when she had no stable home life? Alexa did what she could, but given the demands of her job, that only went so far.

When the girl didn't respond, Alexa gave her another squeeze and asked, "So how are Smith and Wesson?"

Mention of the horses immediately brightened her up. "I fed them and curried them. They're doing fine. I also rode Wesson out down the old mining trail. Poor Smith acted all jealous when we got back."

"Well, you'll have to take Smith out tomorrow."

"Yeah," Stacy giggled. "They always get jealous of one another. Why don't we go riding together?"

"I'll be in Benson."

The mood darkened again. "Oh. Right."

"Sorry. I probably won't have to be there long."

"That's what you always say."

Alexa sighed. Yeah, that is what she always said.

How could she give this kid what she needed when she was gone all the time?

CHAPTER SIX

Downtown Phoenix, the next day

Kurt Billings, Arizona state prosecutor, was having his typical stressful day.

He had a big case coming up in court. The wife of a guy with a meth lab was being tried as an accessory. The husband was already in jail, having been caught red-handed cooking up in the bathroom of a sleazy motel. The wife claimed she knew nothing about it. Records of their texts and social media didn't show anything incriminating, but it didn't take too much intelligence to keep quiet on things like that.

But there was plenty of circumstantial evidence. Material for making meth kept in the garage or in the trunk of the husband's car, which the wife frequently used because her own car got poorer mileage. There was also all the unexplained money that the wife didn't hesitate spending.

So yeah, she was guilty as hell. The problem was proving it beyond a reasonable doubt.

God, he hated that phrase. What it meant was that even if everyone on the jury knew in their gut that the defendant was guilty, they had to let them off if there was any halfway decent argument in the defendant's favor.

Ugh. The public defender in this case was Alexander Zimmerman. One of the best. Good at making criminals look like victims. He'd paint a picture of an innocent, somewhat stupid woman who believed all her husband's lies and would never dream of making dangerous narcotics.

What crap.

Kurt Billings buzzed to the next office to call Hannah, his legal assistant.

"You got those notes typed up yet?"

"Almost, Mr. Billings."

"Almost isn't good enough. Get it done."

Billings shook his head. Slow. Hannah was too damn slow. Granted, typing up notes was the secretary's job, but if he could trust Hannah with anything more complicated, he would.

He really should just fire her. A new graduate of the pre-law program from Arizona State University, he had brought her on board because she had good grades, nice legs, and a serious rack. He thought he could mix work with pleasure.

Fat chance. Every time he got the least bit flirtatious, she'd start talking about her boyfriend, who apparently had a black belt in judo.

She didn't exactly threaten; she was as subtle and as offhand as his advances were. Both of them kept a "reasonable doubt." It was still annoying. He should can her. Can that secretary too. Oh, Geraldine was capable, really capable. It's just that she was pushing sixty. A man's got to have fun in life.

Next he buzzed Jenna.

"Those briefs come in yet?" he demanded.

"They're not supposed to come in for another hour."

Ugh! Surrounded by idiots. He needed a bump.

"Geraldine, I'm busy for the next few minutes. I don't want to be disturbed."

"All right, Mr. Billings."

The state prosecutor opened the bottom left-hand drawer of his desk, rummaged through some stinky old gym clothes he left there so no one would snoop, and pulled out an Altoids tin. Inside was a little mirror, a razor, a rolled up hundred dollar bill, and a baggie of cocaine.

"Huh. Almost out." He reminded himself to call his dealer later. A respectable dealer. One who lived in a decent zip code, who didn't gun down people in the street, and only sold to respectable people who could handle their drugs.

Not like that husband and wife meth team who deserved to go to jail for ten years.

With the same care with which he prepared his series of successful prosecutions, he placed the mirror on his desk, shook out a portion of cocaine, closed and replaced the baggie in the Altoids tin, and began to cut up the cocaine with the razor.

As he did so, he ran through how he was going to convict that white trash meth chick. Basically he'd just railroad her, talk circles around her until she started contradicting herself. She was already upset at what had happened, stressed out by the trial and the loss of her husband

and means of support. It should be easy enough to get her to contradict herself.

That was always a good technique, although you had to be careful. Juries didn't like slick, rich lawyers browbeating defendants. At least not middle-class ones who could put on an air of respectability. This chick, with her country twang, poor diction, and slow responses, wouldn't get much sympathy as long as he didn't come on too strong.

His line was ready. He tightened the roll on the hundred dollar bill and took a single, long sniff.

Sniffling and wiping his nose with the back of his hand, he put away his gear and tucked it under the old socks and shorts, shutting the drawer. That line would kick in within a few minutes.

Now for a coffee at Desert Roast, the nice café down the street, made nicer by that college girl, whatshername, who worked the day shift. Billings had been putting the moves on her for a few days now, ever since she had started working there. Big tips and a few jokes (nothing dirty to scare her off), and compliments about how good she made his coffee. Yeah, he'd get there. And he was always funnier when he'd had a line.

Besides, he needed to get the hell out of this office. He'd never score with anyone here.

* * *

Sitting at the window of a Starbucks across the street, the man who wanted Billings dead waited, and watched.

Billings usually came out of his office at about this time. The last three workdays he had gone to the pricey independent café down the street. The day before that he must have been in a hurry, because his personal assistant had come here into Starbucks to pick him up a coffee.

The man hunting Billings already recognized the personal assistant, and knew she was getting coffee for her boss because she picked up what he always got, a red eye—a regular cup of black coffee with a shot of espresso.

Long hours, stressful job, heavy cocaine use, caffeine addict … that man was heading for a heart attack before he was fifty.

It didn't matter. He wouldn't live long enough to get one.

No, he deserved to die far, far sooner than that.

The man hunting Billings perked up. The state prosecutor had just left the building, taking those long strides he always did when he had just snorted a line or two.

Time to tail him. He kept his Starbucks cup even though it had been empty for twenty minutes. Always good to have a prop. Who would commit a murder with a coffee in his hand?

Billings sped through the downtown crowd, weaving his way between equally hurrying businessmen, younger service workers staring at their phones, and a few shoppers. He nearly tripped over the baby carriage pushed by a woman and cursed under his breath. The woman glared at him, but Billings had already passed. No one paid any attention to the nondescript man with the Starbucks cup walking half a block behind him.

No one paid much attention to anything, the murderer realized. When he had been casing out the homes of the two judges, no one had stopped him despite his having driven through several times, and run through in the evening posing as a jogger.

He had been careful. Most criminals got caught because they slipped up one way or the other. They were drunk or high when they committed the crime, or bragged about it afterwards, or were simply stupid.

He would make none of those mistakes. He would plan his crimes carefully, patiently, and get his revenge on every one of these so-called "upholders of justice."

Caution and patience were of the utmost importance, because the list was very, very long.

As he expected, up ahead he saw Billings enter the Desert Roast. The murderer slowed his pace, giving Billings a bit of time to settle in.

He passed the glass front of the Desert Roast less than a minute later. Inside he saw Billings standing in front of the counter talking loudly and waving his hands in the air as a pretty college-aged barista kept up an awkward smile. Two young guys at a nearby table grinned and pointed at Billings behind his back.

High again, just like he had been at the trial. No wonder Billings had messed up.

He'd pay for that. Oh yes, he'd pay.

The killer paused, muscles tensing. His hand strayed to the clasp knife he had hidden in his pocket. Not as big as he liked, but good enough to do the job. It would be so easy to go in there right now and plunge it right between the prosecutor's shoulder blades as he tried to sweet talk the barista.

No. Not today. If he went in there now he'd only get caught. He had to maintain control. Stick to the plan. This little bit of shadowing had only been to confirm Billings was a man of habit, despite his erratic record in the courtroom. If the state prosecutor kept to his usual schedule, the murderer knew exactly where Billings would be late tonight.

And that's when he'd strike. He had it all planned.

And he planned everything very, very well.

CHAPTER SEVEN

As Alexa predicted, her partner blew down the highway, ignoring the speed limit and weaving between traffic. Twice they ran through speed traps, popular in Arizona as ways for local police departments to raise extra revenue, and both times Stuart got on the police radio installed in the dashboard of his unmarked car and politely told them to get lost.

"You must have been terrifying as a teenager," Alexa said.

"Wrapped my grandma's '82 Nissan Stanza around a tree."

"I didn't need to know that."

"Don't worry. You should have seen me drive a Hummer through Karbala."

"Arizona is rough enough for me."

Stuart turned to her and grinned. "Hanging out with you is rough enough for me too."

"You're going a hundred. Watch the road."

"Anything from the team back in Phoenix?"

"They've been going through the records. Eliminated a bunch from the list but haven't come up with any good suspects."

"Damn."

"They said they'd call immediately if anything came up."

"You don't sound very hopeful."

"That's because I'm not.

"Neither am I. Well, here we are," Stuart said.

A sign said the town was a mile ahead. Stuart slowed, then got down to a respectable 50 mph as they went through Benson, a little settlement of 5,000 people given over mostly to the tourist trade and as a local center for farms, ranches, and mines. They passed a decent-looking motel. Alexa made a mental note of it. They might have to stay here tonight. As a precaution, they had both packed bags and put them in the trunk.

Alexa's bag contained, carefully wrapped in one of Alexa's shirts, Robert Powers's journal. She hadn't had the time to read any the previous night, not with the kid needing cheering up. She'd read some tonight, though.

For some reason, that made her nervous.

"Keeping going straight," Alexa said.

They passed a sign saying, "San Pedro River," then went across a short concrete bridge. Beneath them was a dry wash green with scrub and a few trees clinging to the banks.

"Huh. A river without any water," Stuart said.

"It has water in monsoon season."

"Monsoon season?"

"Wait a bit. Starts every summer around this time. It's actually a bit late this year. Storms come up from Mexico every afternoon and dump a huge amount of water in a couple of hours. The lightning displays are awesome. An hour after it stops, everything is dry again. But you have to be careful. If you get caught in a wash, that's a dry riverbed, you can drown."

"Wow. That should be interesting. I'll try surfing a wash next month."

Alexa chuckled. Then what he had said made her think. Would he be here next month? This collaboration between the U.S. Marshals Service and the FBI was only a temporary experiment. Would he be back East in a month? What would she do for a partner then?

"This used to be a perennial river," Alexa said for something to say. "But the water table has lowered with the rise of population. Too many people sucking out too little water. A hundred years ago this was a proper river. There were even beavers living in it."

"Careful. Canada might invade."

"We'll get you back in your Hummer if that happens. Take a left here. Judge Rodriguez's home is just up that road there."

As planned, they found the local sheriff waiting for them outside a ranch home in a small housing development of scattered houses at the edge of the green area fed by the subsurface damp of the San Pedro. Once Stuart parked behind the sheriff's patrol car and they got out, Alexa breathed in the rich smell of well-watered land. At least well-watered by Arizona's standards.

"Close to a so-called river and we're still in desert," Stuart muttered. Alexa only smiled.

A portly Anglo sheriff walked up to them, hand extended.

"I'm Sheriff Hank Tyson, good to have you on board." Alexa noticed he shook her hand first, and addressed her. Sheriff Tyson knew she was bringing an FBI agent along, and shared many local lawmen's distaste for the feds.

Of course, the U.S. Marshals was a federal agency too, but people in these parts didn't think that way. The Marshals had helped tame this land, long before J. Edgar Hoover created the FBI in Washington.

"Mrs. Rodriguez is inside," the sheriff told them, his face going grim.

"Really?" Alexa was surprised.

"She's a tough lady. Told me this has been her home for twenty-five years and no killer was going to scare her out of it. We got someone watching the place, of course."

Alexa let out a huff of air. She had been hoping to put off meeting the widow.

"Let's go see what we have," she said.

Sheriff Tyson knocked on the front door. After a minute, it was answered by a Hispanic woman in her late fifties. Her movements were stiff, her expression distracted. The sheriff took off his hat, revealing a bald pate.

"Hello, Carmen," the sheriff said. "Sorry to disturb you, but they're here now. This is Deputy U.S. Marshal Alexa Chase and Special Agent Stuart Barrett of the FBI."

"Pleased to meet you. Do come in. Would you like some coffee?" This was said without any intonation whatsoever. The poor woman was running on automatic.

"That would be great, Carmen," the sheriff said quietly.

They came to the living room, brightly decorated with flowers and photos of family on both sides of the border. The mantlepiece was covered with sympathy cards in English and Spanish. The coffee table groaned under the weight of an array of cakes, preserves, and home-baked bread. A large cooler sat in the corner.

Carmen Rodriguez moved to a side table where there was a hot plate and a coffeepot.

"I'm afraid I can't make it properly, but I'm not supposed to go in the kitchen. That's where it happened. Hank, you still take cream? I know the doctor told you no more sugar. And how would you two like it?"

Still that automatic, almost robotic speech. This woman was in shock.

She shouldn't be staying here, Alexa thought. *But who am I to tell her to leave her home?*

"With cream, thank you Mrs. Rodriguez," Alexa said.

"Black, ma'am," Stuart said.

"Feel free to help yourselves to the food on the coffee table. Everyone came with something. Far more than I could ever eat."

Alexa wondered if this woman had eaten anything since coming back to a murdered husband. Alexa didn't touch any of the food. Neither did the two men.

Carmen got to work on the coffee. The silence lengthened. Sheriff Tyson glanced at Alexa, who took a deep breath and asked,

"Do you know anyone who might want to harm your husband?"

Carmen gave a little shrug. "Hank asked me all these questions before, but I guess you need to ask again. As I said, there are lots of people. Antonio put away a lot of bad people over the years. Murderers, arsonists, the head of a child pornography ring, coyotes—those are the men who bring illegals over the border—a team of bank robbers, gang members. All kinds."

"Can you think of anyone in particular?"

"I don't know," Carmen said and let out a little sigh, the first sign of emotion in this burnt-out woman. "He sat on the bench for so long. Many of the people he put in jail must be out by now."

"Has anyone threatened him?"

"A few times over the years. No one recently."

Sheriff Tyson cut in. "I sat down with Antonio's assistant and wrote up a list of names of criminals who threatened him. Oh, and there was also the egg throwing incident."

"What was that?" Stuart asked.

"A couple of years ago, Antonio had to let a local killer off for lack of evidence. This hitchhiker had been spotted close to the scene of a local girl who had been strangled. I arrested him. Searched him and found nothing of the girl's in his possession. He did have a big wad of cash, though. The girl had just cashed a check and was known to be carrying a large amount of cash that had been stolen off the body. That was enough for him to go to trial. A few witnesses came forward, but the public defender poked holes in all their stories. It was a typical case of people believing what they wanted to believe."

"So Judge Rodriguez let him go?" Alexa asked.

Sheriff Tyson nodded. "I think it was the right decision. I think that guy stole the money from somewhere, he was a drifter, but there was no evidence he got it from her. He claimed to have won the money gambling. I grilled him pretty hard and he held up to all of it. My gut said he wasn't our man and the CSI boys couldn't find anything linking him to the crime scene. I'd bet a thousand dollars he was innocent."

"But the public didn't see it that way," Stuart said.

Carmen Rodriguez turned from making the coffee. "Jed Fisher led a mob here to protest. Threw eggs at the house. There must have been a dozen people outside. Hank came and cleared them out, gave them all a fine."

The sheriff nodded. "Also gave him a warning for dragging the judge's name through the mud on social media. That quieted him some."

"Has he ever had a run-in with Judge Warburton in Phoenix?"

"No. But I heard his cousin just got locked up in Phoenix for drunk and disorderly. Might have been that judge. I can't recall."

I know what my bet is on.

"Have you spoken to Mr. Fisher?" Alexa asked.

"No. I was waiting for the two of you. I figure three of us from three different agencies will put the scare in him. We'll go down to the San Pedro Café in a minute and talk to him."

"You know he's there?" Alexa asked.

The sheriff snorted. "He's always there, drinking coffee in the mornings and beer in the afternoons. Then he goes to the roadhouse and drinks whiskey. That man hasn't worked a day in his life, unless causing trouble counts as work."

Carmen served the coffee.

"Thank you for the coffee, ma'am," Stuart said, "but I think we should be going to get this Jed character."

"Don't worry about him," the sheriff replied. "He's too lazy to leave town, and my deputy reported he was at his usual stool not half an hour ago."

Alexa was itching to go too, but they were on the sheriff's territory.

Always listen to the local law, especially if they've been working the job a while and are from the community, Powers told her once. *They'll know the area better than anyone.*

"We should probably go check," Stuart said. Then turned to the widow. "Sorry you had to make coffee for nothing, ma'am, but this case is very urgent."

"I understand." Carmen went to a side table and pulled out three plastic cups. She poured their coffees into them.

"I don't want you to go emptyhanded," she said. "Are you sure you don't want any cake?"

Stuart looked abashed. "No, thank you ma'am. We'll need to go now."

They gave their condolences to the widow at the door. When she closed it, Alexa had the impression of a tomb being sealed.

As they walked to the cars, Stuart said in a low voice, "She shouldn't be staying there. She's messing up a crime scene. Bad for her mental health too."

The sheriff cocked an eyebrow. "Why don't you go back and tell her that?"

Stuart gave a little shrug and looked away.

They pulled out of the parking lot and followed the sheriff's car back downtown.

"I'll take us to the next street over so we can park without Jed seeing us," Sheriff Tyson told them over the police radio.

They parked on a dusty street lined with a dollar store, a laundromat, and several boarded up shops. Then they circled around the block on foot and came to the San Pedro Café. To the east, both streets ended after about a hundred yards at the banks of the river, marked by a screen of trees and vegetation. The bridge spanning it was a couple of blocks away.

It was a long cafeteria in the old style, with windows going along the front giving a view inside of a long counter, a row of stools upholstered with faded red leather, and several booths. Behind the counter was a soda machine, a large refrigerator for beer, and a grill where a stocky woman was making hamburgers. Two men, one small and the other husky, sat together at the counter with their backs to the window. An old man in a John Deere hat sipped his coffee cup alone in a booth. Two teenagers lounged in another booth, laughing loudly enough to be heard through the glass.

"Jed Fisher is the smaller man at the counter," the sheriff said. "Let me talk to him."

As they got to the glass door, one of the teenagers elbowed his friend. They turned to stare at the sheriff and his two companions.

When the teen belted out a laugh and spoke, they heard it clearly.

"Aw, Jed, you're in for it now!"

Jed turned around, showing a grizzled face and wide eyes under the brim of a Phoenix Suns cap. He leapt off the stool and ran for a back hallway next to the counter.

CHAPTER EIGHT

Stuart rushed through the door after Jed Fisher. Over the cackling of the teenagers, he heard the sheriff shout, "I'll circle around and cut him off!" He didn't know if Alexa followed him or the sheriff; he was too busy chasing this hayseed.

He blew past the hefty man Jed had been sitting with, who didn't move an inch, only watched, and ducked into the back hallway into which Jed had disappeared. As he suspected, past a men's and women's bathrooms was another door at the back wall of the café. Jed wrenched it open and darted out before Stuart could stop him.

They ended up in a narrow alley, the heat from the noonday sun feeling even worse after briefly being in an airconditioned interior. Jed bolted down a dusty alley past the blank backs of a couple of buildings with faded yellow paint, then hooked a right. Stuart followed, only a few paces behind him.

The FBI agent rounded the corner, taking a longer route in case Jed spun around and tried to jump him.

But the guy was still running.

Damn fast for someone who sits on a barstool all day.

"FBI! Stop and put your hands up!" Stuart shouted.

Jed ignored him, taking a left onto the street where Stuart and the sheriff had just parked. Stuart picked up speed, sweat breaking out on his skin.

Damn. It's as hot as Iraq out here! I should have asked for a posting in Maine or someplace. At least I'm not wearing a helmet and Kevlar.

Hope I don't need them for this guy.

Stuart thought of pulling his gun but didn't want to slow his rhythm. He was beginning to gain on the suspect.

A brief glance over his shoulder showed Alexa coming out of the alley, and the sheriff just rounding the far corner of the building.

Good job cutting him off, sheriff. You should have brought your horse.

Stuart faced forward and concentrated on reducing the distance between him and Jed Fisher. It looked like the guy was headed for that line of trees and bushes. Maybe he thought he could lose him there. Maybe he could.

Catch him now so you don't have to find out.

They passed the laundromat, where an elderly Hispanic woman stared openmouthed at them through the grubby window, and right by a lone man in a cowboy hat who stood, hands in pockets, watching them with no apparent interest. Stuart half expected him to spit tobacco juice on Stuart's dress shoes.

He was almost on Jed now. The trees were just a few yards ahead. Jed took a quick glance over his shoulder and put a hand in his pocket.

Stuart immediately stopped and got to one knee, pulling out his gun in a single fluid motion.

"Hands up!"

But Jed wasn't going for a gun, and he wasn't stopping. He threw something into the underbrush as he entered the vegetation. Stuart had a glimpse of a small plastic bag.

Stuart leapt up and rushed after, holstering his pistol. This guy wasn't armed, and it was best not to be carrying a gun in your hand when you tackled someone. The gun could go off or, even worse, they might decide to fight you for it.

Instead he'd pummel this guy into submission.

He had to catch him first. Panting, sweat pouring down his face now and stinging his eyes, Stuart entered the cool shade of the low trees, desert grass swishing against his legs.

Just a few yards ahead, Jed hurried down the embankment of the San Pedro River.

As Stuart reached the edge of the rocky, sandy slope, he saw Jed a few feet below, cartwheeling his arms to stay upright as he ran down the steep incline toward the dry riverbank of sand and windblown trash.

Stuart launched himself in the air, reaching his arms wide and hitting the suspect with a football tackle from behind. His arms went around Jed's middle, and together they rolled down the slope, Stuart timing it perfectly so that when they reached the bottom, Jed was beneath him, face down in an old empty supersized bag of potato chips.

Spitting out some sand and blinking the sweat from his eyes, Stuart pinned him with a knee to the small of his back, pulled out a pair of cuffs, and got Jed's hands behind his back.

The perp managed to raise his face out of the old wrapper.

"You'll never take me alive, you son of a bitch!"

"I just did," Stuart gasped. He wanted to add something witty and cutting, but he was too tired to think of anything.

Stuart stood, wiped his brow with the back of his sleeve, which only stained his suit and put more sand on his face, then pulled Jed up onto his feet.

"You run pretty good for a cop," Jed grumbled.

"College football. You?"

"Track and field in high school. I'd have beat you if I wasn't hung over."

"Whatever. Let's go."

"You scuffed them pretty shoes, city boy," Jed said.

"Never mind that. We got some questions for you."

They worked their way up the slope. Alexa and the sheriff appeared at the top.

"Nice of you to join us," Stuart said. "He threw a little plastic bag into the underbrush."

"I'll bet you ten dollars I know what's in it," Sheriff Tyson said.

"I'm not taking that bet," Stuart huffed. "God, it's hot."

The sheriff went off to search the underbrush as Alexa came up to him.

"You all right?"

"Still one of the greatest linesmen ever to graduate from Penn State."

Alexa turned to Jed. "You know why we wanted you?"

"I don't know nothing, and I didn't do nothing."

"Anything," Stuart corrected. "You didn't do anything."

"That's what I said. I didn't do nothing."

Stuart sighed. "Never mind."

Stuart handed Jed over to Alexa and started dusting off his suit.

I wonder if I can put the dry cleaning on expenses?

"Bingo!" Sheriff Tyson called, standing up amid a clump of tall grass and holding a baggie up high.

"Aw, crap," Jed muttered.

The sheriff strolled over. Stuart could see it was filled with small white crystals.

"Well, well, well, a nice little haul of crystal meth," the sheriff said. "Don't you know this junk is bad for your teeth?"

"That ain't mine," Jed said.

"Yes it is," all three officers said at the same time.

The sheriff read him his rights and they headed back to the café.

"Why did those kids warn you?" Stuart asked.

Jed said nothing.

"You know them?" Stuart asked the sheriff.

"I do. We'll have a word."

"They'll be long gone."

"I don't think so."

The sheriff turned out to be right. As they came to the café, they saw the old man in the John Deere hat standing out front, holding both teens by the wrist. The kids looked downcast and nervous, even though they stood a foot taller and must have weighed at least 30 pounds more than the thin old man.

"Hey, Clyde. Looks like you gone fishing and caught two big ones," the sheriff called, then turned to Stuart and Alexa. "Clyde's the math teacher at the high school."

"We didn't do nothing!" one of the kids protested.

"Anything," Clyde corrected.

In a voice that carried authority but wasn't unkind, the sheriff said, "How about you two kids go back to your booth? I want to talk to Jed a minute. And don't move a muscle or I'll call your parents."

"Yes, sir," they muttered, and went back inside.

"Need me for anything more?" Clyde asked.

"Naw, that's OK. Just think up some excuse to give them Saturday morning detention for the next four weeks."

"Will do." Clyde strolled off.

"If those kids have drugs on them, they'll ditch them," Stuart whispered.

"They don't have drugs on them," the sheriff said.

"But—"

The sheriff looked him in the eye. "They don't have drugs on them."

Stuart glanced through the window. The boys were back in the booth, sitting slumped and half out of sight, but not out of sight enough to hide the fact that one of them was reaching into his pants.

No point in chasing it if the local law wants to look the other way, Stuart thought. *We got a murder to solve.*

And maybe that math teacher can fix it better than the law.

Still, it nettled him. He tried to focus on the sheriff as he began to question Jed.

"So I know you heard about Judge Rodriguez."

Jed paled. "Is that what this is about?"

Stuart studied him. Was this an act? Of course everyone always acted surprised when faced with charges, like kids caught by their teacher cheating on a test.

"Uh-huh. Now, you and him have a little history," the sheriff said.

"I ain't never been in his court in my life."

"No, but you've been in courts in Tucson, Bisbee, and Alamogordo. And I wasn't talking about that. I was talking about that little egg throwing incident a while back."

Jed's face turned red. "He let Diane's murderer go free!"

"There was no evidence and you know it. You've been talking bad about the judge ever since."

Jed shook his head. "I wouldn't kill him. You know I didn't like him but I'm no killer."

The sheriff snorted. "Just a drug dealer and petty thief."

And you sure got angry when the sheriff brought up that acquittal.

"A man's got to live," Jed protested.

Stuart rolled his eyes. He hated it when criminals used the poverty excuse. In his platoon he had men and women from the Appalachians and the Hood. They were born into poverty too, and took the Army as a way out of it. They made something of themselves.

At least the ones who came back.

"So where were you at around ten to midnight on the night of July 3?"

Jed thought for a moment. A mark in his favor in Stuart's eyes. Suspects who were quick with their answers were the ones who already had something prepared. Ask a regular person that same question, and they always have to think.

The smart cons know that, though, and always playact.

"I was … wait, that was Saturday? Oh, I was playing cards with Ben Greenstone, Peter Andreson, and Ike Tallen."

"A fine crowd of model citizens. If I ask them will they tell me you were there?"

"Of course they will," he said, glancing through the window to look inside the café. "Oh, and I went to the AM / PM Minimart to pick up a twelve pack around midnight. We ran out."

"So you had already been drinking and went to AM / PM to keep the party going?"

Jed's eyes got shifty. "They were drinking."

"Riiight. I know Georgine keeps the tapes for a whole week, so I'll go have a looksee."

"You do that."

"Stay here with the feds while I go inside."

Despite not being invited, Stuart joined him. After that chase, he needed some air conditioning.

The cold interior hit him like a plate glass wall. He shivered a little, grabbed some napkins from the counter, and started wiping his face and hands.

"Please don't get sand on my floor," the woman behind the counter said. "I just mopped."

"Sorry," Stuart said.

The teens scooted down lower in their booth. Sheriff Tyson ignored them and addressed the hefty man who had been sitting next to Jed.

"Hey, Ike. What were you doing on Saturday night?"

"Playing cards and drinking with Jed and a couple of others."

"Did Jed leave at any time in the evening."

"Yeah. We run out of beer and he went out to get more."

"Do you know where?"

"No. I figure the AM / PM. It's the closest to my place."

"When did he leave?"

Ike shrugged.

"How long was he gone?"

"About twenty minutes. Yeah, so he must have gone to the AM / PM. The Circle K on the highway is too far for him to get back so quick."

"Thanks, Ike."

The woman behind the counter handed Stuart a glass of water, which he drained with a heartfelt thank you.

The sheriff and Stuart stepped a little apart.

"I think Ike's telling the truth," Sheriff Tyson said in a low voice.

"Yeah," Stuart whispered back. "If Jed had prompted him, he would have given the time."

"And the AM / PM is the opposite direction from Ike's place than the judge's home.

"We need to check those tapes."

"Yeah. I'm going to have another word with Jed."

The sheriff stepped out. Stuart clicked his tongue. This looked like a dead end.

Damn.

Stuart glanced over at the teenagers. They were still shifting around, hunkered low in their seats.

When they noticed him watching, they stared back at him, looking as guilty as hell.

I can't leave this.

Taking a deep breath, he walked over to the teenagers.

CHAPTER NINE

He strolled over to the booth with the two teenagers. Their eyes went as round as saucers.

"Crammed between the cushions or under the next booth?" Stuart asked.

"Huh?"

"Don't play dumb. Although if you're hanging out with a guy like that it's convincing enough."

He sat down on the same seat they were both on, making them move over.

"What are you, a pedo?" one of the kids asked. His friend snickered.

"No, I'm an FBI agent."

He tossed his ID onto the table. The kids stopped snickering.

Stuart pulled out his phone and brought up the DEA website.

"Every heard of meth mouth?" he asked.

"Huh?" the kids said.

"What happens if you take meth for a while. Check this out."

As part of their public outreach program, the DEA had set up a site showing before and after pictures of meth addicts, with dates when the photos were taken. Stuart started scrolling through them. Photo after photo of young, attractive people who a year later had wrinkled, sagging skin, dead eyes, and rotted teeth.

"Meth is the best high there is, or so they tell me," Stuart said. "Blows your mind but wrecks your body. Within a month you won't be able to play any sports. Within two months you won't want to. In a year you'll look as old as your dad, and uglier."

He kept scrolling through the pictures. The two teens kept quiet, staring.

After a moment, one of them piped up, "But that only happens to addicts."

"Happens quicker to addicts. But each time you use it, even if you only use it from time to time, you'll start to look like these guys."

"They're Photoshopped," the kid said in a tone that sounded like he was trying to convince himself.

"Hey, this guy looks like you." Stuart zoomed in on a decayed mouth surrounded by slack lips. "Or at least he used to."

"Gross. He probably never brushes his teeth."

"Probably not. You forget stuff like that on meth. Forget to wipe your ass too."

A pair of teenage boys should have laughed at that, but for some reason they were no longer in a laughing mood.

Stuart reached behind the nearest one.

"Hey! What are you doing?"

Stuart stuffed his hand between the cushion and backrest, rooted around through the crumbs and dust, and pulled out a small baggie of white crystals.

The teenagers froze.

"Where did you get this?"

"It isn't ours," one kid said.

"Where did you get this?" Stuart growled.

"You can't prove it's ours."

"I can if I take it to a fingerprint lab. Or you can tell me where you got this."

The two looked at each other for a moment. One raised his eyebrows and bugged out his eyes. The other shook his head. One slugged the other in the shoulder.

"All riiiight!"

"Then say it."

"You say it."

"No, you say it."

"How about you both say it," Stuart suggested.

"Jed," the first kid said.

"Some guy at the gas station," the other said at the same time.

They looked at each other.

"So which is it?" Stuart asked.

The one who claimed he bought it at the gas station hung his head.

"Jed," he said in an almost inaudible tone.

The sheriff walked back into the café and approached the table. Stuart held up the baggie of crystal meth. The sheriff's face fell, making Stuart confused.

"We can bust Jed Fisher for dealing now," Stuart explained.

One of the kids blurted, "He made us take it. We were going to throw it away, Uncle Hank. Honest!"

Whoops.

The sheriff turned beet red.

At least now I know why you were so reluctant. The next family reunion is going to be pretty awkward.

The sheriff couldn't quite look him in the eye as he said, "I'll, um, take their statements."

Suddenly, Stuart felt guilty. "You know, they might be right about Jed forcing it on them. Back where I came from, there was this local dealer who would push drugs on the high school kids. I always avoided him. He was a bully, just like Jed Fisher, right boys?"

The kids brightened.

"Yeah! He threatened to beat us up if we told," one kid said.

I believe it.

The other kid added, "Yeah, we tried to avoid him, like you said, but he chased us and forced us to take that meth."

That not so much.

The sheriff looked from one kid to the other, baffled.

Stuart raised his hands. "You see? They're clearly terrified of him. That's why they warned Jed. If they hadn't, they would have had to face his wrath."

"What's wrath?" one kid asked.

"It's like, a ghost or something," his friend told him.

"That's a wraith, dummy."

"Who are you calling a dummy?"

"You!"

"You're the one who took the meth!"

"He made us, remember?"

"Yeah. Um, right."

Stuart cut them off before they could demonstrate any more of their stupidity.

"So you see, sheriff, they weren't at fault. Two innocent boys, practically children, terrorized by the bully of the town. We shouldn't book them. We would only be blaming the victims."

"You think?" the sheriff asked, obviously confused at being offered a lifeline from a fed holding a bag of meth in his hand.

"Sure. Why don't you process Jed and we'll meet you back at the station, OK?"

"Right."

The sheriff gave the two teens a long glare. They wilted. Then the sheriff turned on his heel and stalked out.

Stuart turned to the two boys. "Give me your phone numbers and home addresses."

"Why?" one asked.

"Because I told you to," Stuart snapped.

They gave it to him. He texted both to check they were legit and made them put his number in their address book.

"Now then, what year are you in?"

"We're sophomores."

"You're fifteen?"

"Yeah."

Jesus Christ.

"OK, here's the deal. I'm going to check on you from time to time. If you don't answer my call promptly, I'm coming down here. If I hear from the sheriff that you've gotten in trouble, I'm coming down here. If I hear from Clyde that you're failing or causing trouble in school, I'm coming down here. And you do *not* want me coming down here."

"Um, OK." The kids looked as confused as "Uncle Hank."

Stuart went on.

"If you stay out of trouble and graduate, you can call me. I'll help you get into college or get a job. You can get out of this hick town. I grew up in a small town like this and I would have loved someone to help me get out of it. The word of an FBI agent can open a lot of doors. It's your choice. Screw up again and end up like Jed Fisher, or keep it cool and get a leg up in life."

Stuart got up and walked out of the café. Alexa waited for him just outside.

"Give them a good talking to?" she asked with a smile.

"They were almost young enough to giving a spanking to."

"Not sure you could get away with that."

"No," he said with a grin.

"Well if you're done, we'll go look at that camera footage."

Stuart nodded.

Yeah, let's get going. I have a feeling it's going to be a dead end. We need to get to work on this case in a hurry. That killer might be looking for Number Three.

CHAPTER TEN

Four hours later, Alexa put down the phone in the Benson Police Department's work room and sighed in disgust. As she expected, the convenience store camera showed Jed Fisher buying a 24 pack of Budweiser almost at the exact same time as the murder, and a good twenty-minutes' drive away. That and the testimony of three eyewitnesses, plus his own stubborn denial, pretty much eliminated him from suspicion.

So she and Stuart had stayed in Benson, calling parole officers and ex-cons from the intimidatingly long list of people who had been processed by both judges. She had never fully realized just how often career criminals got tried in multiple courts.

One after another, these less-than-model citizens came up clean. A few had died. Some were back in jail. Some had tight alibis from their parole officers. Some didn't even live the Southwest anymore.

At least Stuart had the chance to send his suit to the local dry cleaners and change into his spare suit—an identical black one that was equally unsuitable for Arizona in July. She needed to talk to him about that.

She leaned back, closing her eyes to rest them and stretching her arms over her head. This endless round of calls was exhausting.

The grunt work isn't glamorous, Robert used to say, *but nine times out of ten it's what gets your man.*

A wave of sadness washed over her over the loss of her partner. It hit her at odd times, coming out of nowhere. In the mornings she'd wake up, brew some coffee, and go out back to feed Smith and Wesson. She'd breathe in the fresh morning air of the Sonora Desert and watch the sunrise. Then she'd remember Robert was dead and the sunrise didn't look so beautiful anymore, and her horses couldn't cheer her up. At those times, nothing helped and only work gave her a sense of purpose.

That and taking care of Stacy.

But the kid would have to take care of herself today, and Alexa needed to get back to work.

Just as she brought up the next file in her computer, her phone rang. Looking at the number, she saw it was Joan, her therapist. Marshal Hernandez had quietly insisted that she see one to "work through the pain of losing Marshal Powers." He hadn't actually said it was a condition for her returning to work, but the implication had been clear enough.

Most likely it was the beating that had prompted it. On her last case, the serial killer Drake Logan had sent someone to murder her. The thug had managed to slash her with a knife before she knocked him down. Then she had proceeded to beat the living daylights out of him. The video a passerby took went viral. What could have been another media storm got headed off when Marshal Hernandez revealed who had sent the guy. The country was already horrified by Drake Logan's escape and new round of murders, and quickly forgave a Deputy Marshal who had been a bit overzealous in defending herself.

Marshal Hernandez knew the truth, though. She had gone over the line because she was near her mental breaking point.

Alexa's phone was still ringing. She picked up, not wanting Joan to think she was ignoring her, as much as she'd have liked to.

"Hello, Joan."

"Hi, Alexa, how are you doing?" Joan's voice was calm, soothing. In their first and so far only meeting, she had shown herself to be attentive, a good listener. Caring. Unfortunately, she had never served in the military or law enforcement, so she had absolutely no idea what Alexa was going through. Couldn't they have found a therapist with a bit of life experience?

"I'm doing well."

"Have you tried the breathing exercises we discussed last time?"

"Oh, um. Sure." *Breathing exercises? I forgot all about that.* "Yes, I think they're helping."

"That's great, Alexa. Really great. When can I expect to see you?"

Alexa looked at the clock on the wall, her heart sinking. She was supposed to have a second therapy session today, starting five minutes ago.

"I'm sorry, Joan. I totally forgot to call you. I'm in Benson on a case. It came up at the last minute."

"That's perfectly all right, Alexa. Just keep me informed, all right?"

"Yeah. Sorry."

"When should I pencil you in?"

"Um, I'm not sure exactly. Let me give you a call."

"All right. I understand how your job can give you an unpredictable schedule. How did the last few days go for you since we had our meeting?"

Alexa paused, the trauma of seeing the Jersey Devil hitting her again full force. She closed her eyes, took a deep breath and said,

"It was good. Relaxing. I spent a lot of time riding."

Her voice must have betrayed her, because Joan asked, "Any major stressors?"

The honest answer welled up in her throat. Alexa pushed it back down. She wasn't ready to talk about it. At least not yet. And certainly not over the phone.

"It's been a struggle dealing with losing Robert," she admitted, hearing her voice crack. "Sometimes I go for fifteen minutes or even an hour without thinking about it, especially if I'm working or hanging out with Stacy, and then it hits me."

"That's a normal part of the grieving process. The breathing exercises will help you get over the worst of the panic reactions."

"Thanks. Um, I really need to go now. This case is very time sensitive. This guy has already killed two judges and he might go after another."

"All right, Alexa. Call me as soon as you can and don't forget to do the breathing exercises."

Alexa hung up, still trying to remember how those damn breathing exercises went.

She grimaced. Joan was a good person and was only trying to help, but talking about losing your partner and mentor wasn't going to make it any easier. Drake's men had cut his head off right in front of her. Breathing exercises weren't going to help with that.

When you're feeling down, remember that we make a difference, Robert had told her more than once.

"OK, let's call this guy's parole officer," she muttered to herself.

Just then, Stuart burst in. "I got a lead!"

Alexa leapt up. "Great! Let's go get him."

Stuart took a step back. "Whoa! You're eager. I said a lead, not a solid suspect."

Alexa flushed. She was so desperate to get her mind off things by getting back on the case, she had acted like a fool.

"So what do you have?" she asked in a calmer voice.

“Nathaniel White got sent to prison by Judge Rodriguez for four years for assault and battery plus theft. The guy had some argument with a neighbor and beat him up with a tire iron, then stole a bunch of money he had on him. White was incarcerated in Phoenix. When he first came up for parole, Judge Warburton got the case and turned him down. Apparently he had been beating up fellow inmates and stealing their commissary.”

“Nice guy.”

“It gets better. Or worse. He’s out now, supposedly living in Phoenix but he hasn’t checked in with his parole officer for two weeks.”

“Any leads on where he might be?”

“The parole officer gave me an address of his girlfriend, who lives in Marana. That’s just a little north of Tucson.”

“I know. I’m surprised you do.”

Stuart grinned. “Hey, you got me driving all over this state. All I have to do is pay attention to the road signs.”

“Let’s go check out the girlfriend.”

“Right. We’ll swing by the dry cleaners on the way out of town. I’ll be happy to see the last of this place. Oh, let’s get a coffee too. I didn’t want to get one here in case the sheriff spat in it.”

* * *

By the time they got to Marana, a town of 45,000 about 20 miles northwest of Tucson, the sun had set and the western sky was fading into a deep blue. They got off Interstate 10 and headed through pecan groves and some cotton fields, Stuart glancing curiously at the sign of agriculture in the desert.

The pecans were OK, the cotton not so much. Cotton was a thirsty plant, and it bothered Alexa to see such a waste of water in a region where water had always been scarce.

His phone, sitting on the dashboard, lit up with a message. He looked at it. Alexa hated it when he broke the speed limit and checked his phone at the same time. It was something Stacy would do if she was old enough to drive.

“About time they got back to me,” he said. “The local P.D. checked in on the girlfriend, Linda Shepherd, after Nathaniel White skipped his second meeting with his parole officer. She claims she hasn't seen him. They didn't find any evidence he was there."

"How long ago was that?"

"Day before yesterday."

"He might be hiding somewhere a little less obvious. She might know something, though."

Stuart nodded. "People often thumb their nose at the local cops. Getting confronted by two feds makes them think again."

"I'm not a fed."

Stuart looked at her curiously. "The U.S. Marshals is a federal agency."

"Not really."

"What are you talking about? It's the oldest federal law enforcement agency in the country."

"Well, I suppose," Alexa said reluctantly. "If you want to look at it that way."

Stuart laughed, then drawled, "Oh, what you mean is that you're not some damn city slicker from Washington."

"That was a terrible attempt at a Southern accent. What I mean is that I don't wear black suits and no hat in hundred-degree weather."

"Har har."

They turned onto a side street lined with run-down homes with dirt yards littered with broken bicycles, discarded toys, and other trash.

"Does this Linda Shepherd have a record?" Alexa asked.

"No, although I have a feeling she's about to get one." He checked the map on his phone. "Her place is right up ahead. According the Marana P.D., that house on the right has been split into two apartments. Linda Shepherd lives upstairs."

They parked in a gravel drive behind an old Chevy. Stuart checked his phone again and said, "That's her vehicle."

It was the only one in the drive.

"Does Nathaniel White have a vehicle registered in his name?" Alexa asked.

"No. And it looks like the downstairs neighbors are out. We got her and maybe him."

"I'll take the lead on this," Alexa said. Women were sometimes more open with a female officer than a male one.

"All right," Stuart said.

As they passed by Linda's car, Alexa noticed it was covered in dust and had four flat tires. Alexa and Stuart traded a look and continued to the house.

Downstairs the lights were all off, but along the side of the house ran a set of stairs up to a side door and the upstairs apartment. There the lights were on, shining through white curtains. A shadow passed by one of the windows.

Alexa walked up the stairs, Stuart just behind her.

She knocked and put her ear to the door. Sounds of movement inside, and the low babble of a TV. She knocked again. No answer.

Alexa knocked a third time.

"U.S. Marshal. Open up!" she called.

More movement inside. Stuart had placed himself to the side of the door, his hand inside his jacket and touching the holster of his weapon. Alexa gave him a calming gesture.

Considering all the bloodshed in our last case, I can't blame him for being nervous.

She didn't worry about her partner, though. He was cool under fire. Two tours of duty in Iraq had made sure of that. The only time she had seen him rattled was when he nearly got blown up by a bomb. Fair enough.

"Coming!" a female voice came from inside.

The door opened and Alexa saw a woman in her twenties wearing a dirty t-shirt and sweatpants. Her blonde hair was rumpled. The TV played a gameshow in the background.

Alexa looked her in the eye. The woman looked away.

"Linda Shepherd?"

"Yes."

"I'm Deputy Marshal Alexa Chase and this is Special Agent Stuart Barrett of the FBI. We're looking for Nathaniel White."

Linda's eyes went wide. "What for?"

"We just want to talk to him."

Linda looked at the floor and shifted her weight from one foot to the other. "I don't know where he is."

"You sure about that?" Alexa asked.

"Yeah. I haven't seen Nat in a couple of weeks."

"Now, Mrs. White, lying to an officer of the law is a crime."

Linda hung her head lower than Stacy that time she forgot to close the stable door and Wesson ended up eating the neighbor's flowers.

"I haven't seen him," Linda said faintly.

A window opened somewhere in the apartment, followed by the sound of movement and a man cursing.

"Stand aside!" Alexa ordered, pushing past Linda and rushing into the apartment.

She followed the sound through the living room and into a short hallway. She ducked into a bedroom, then heard a noise from the room just down the hall.

Bursting into this room, she saw it was a bathroom. A man was climbing over the toilet, squeezing through an open window.

CHAPTER ELEVEN

"Stop right there!" Alexa ordered.

Nathaniel White ignored her. He was already halfway out the window. Alexa had no idea if there was a sheer drop or a rooftop on the other side of that window. It didn't matter. This guy wasn't getting away.

Alexa grabbed him by the belt, braced one foot against the wall, and hauled him back inside, his head banging against the window.

"Ow! You bitch!"

Nathaniel swung around, his elbow connecting with Alexa's jaw.

She stumbled, the small of her back jamming against the sink.

Nathaniel White stood at least six two, with a glowering face, a scar down one cheek, and muscles everywhere.

A meaty fist swung at Alexa's face.

She dodged just in time so that his fist missed her by less than an inch and smashed into the mirror behind her.

He let out a howl. Alexa gave him an uppercut to the point of the jaw while sweeping his leg. Nathaniel lost his balance, staggered back, and fell into the tub, taking the shower curtain with him, the curtain rod snapping and falling too.

He smacked his head against the tile, but despite this he still thrashed in the tub, his damaged hand smearing blood on the curtain and tile.

Alexa whipped out her extendible baton, opened it with a flick of the wrist, and hit him square on the knee just as he was trying to rise.

Nathaniel let out a string of curses, clutching his knee, his teeth clenched in pain.

"You bitch! I'm going to kill you."

The hulking man tried to rise again. Alexa smacked him in the shoulder, making him lose his grip on the side of the tub and sending him back down again.

"Freeze!"

Stuart was at the door, pointing his gun at Nathaniel's head.

The ex-con let muttered a curse and slowly raised his hands.

"Oh, come on, Mr. White," Stuart said. "You listen to me and not the female officer? That's sexist! You know how hurtful that is? Now she feels marginalized."

"Not marginalized, pissed off," Alexa said, feeling around her teeth with her tongue. They all seemed to be there, although her jaw throbbed like hell.

"Don't they give prisoners sensitivity training in this flyover state?" Stuart asked.

"Quit screwing around and check on the girlfriend," Alexa said, cuffing Nathaniel and helping him out of the tub.

"Meek as a lamb. She hasn't gone anywhere." Stuart walked out to the living room.

"Assaulting an officer of the law is going to get you back in prison where you belong," Alexa said, pushing the convict out of the bathroom. "But I have some more important things to ask you about."

They headed back to the living room, to find Stuart making a search and Linda sitting with her head bowed on the sofa. The game show was still on. Someone had just won the jackpot. Lights flashed and a middle-aged woman jumped up and down, clapping her hands with glee.

"Joint in the ashtray. I'll look in the bedroom while you question Mr. Jailbird."

Stuart headed to the next room.

"Sit," Alexa ordered.

Nathaniel sat on the sofa, wincing as he bent his knee.

"My hand's bleeding. Aren't you going to treat it?" he demanded.

"In a minute. First tell me what you've been doing for the past two weeks and why you haven't talked to your parole officer."

The former and future prisoner shrugged. "I had stuff to do."

"Like?"

"Wanted to see my girl."

"Have you been here the entire time?"

"Yeah."

Alexa looked at Linda, who turned to Nathaniel.

"Don't look at him, look at me," Alexa ordered.

"He's been here the whole two weeks," Linda mumbled, looking at the floor instead. Alexa got the impression that down was her favorite place to look.

"You haven't gone anywhere?"

“My car hasn’t worked for three months,” Linda said.

“I took the bus down here,” Nathaniel said.

“You’re supposed to inform your parole officer if you leave town.”

“Screw him.”

“Why didn’t you check in with him?”

“I got busy.”

“Busy watching gameshows and smoking weed?” Stuart said, coming back into the room with a bag of marijuana.

Alexa turned to the FBI agent. “Stay here with him. I want to speak with her privately.”

“I’ll fix his hand and call this in to the local P.D.,” Stuart said, pulling out a compact first aid kit he kept in his pocket.

Alexa walked with Linda out onto the landing of the staircase and closed the door behind her. A couple of neighbors stood on the sidewalk staring at the house, no doubt attracted by all the noise. When they saw Alexa’s uniform they made themselves scarce. It was that kind of neighborhood.

She turned to Linda and sized her up for a moment. According to the Marana police department, this woman didn’t have a record. But now they could pin her with harboring a fugitive and possession of a controlled substance.

But Alexa didn’t want to do that. She’d met plenty of women like this in her time in law enforcement. Weak, lonely women who cling to bad men because they give them attention and a bit of excitement in their gray little lives. Considering Nathaniel’s nature, Linda might even be battered. Alexa didn’t see any bruises, but that didn’t mean he wasn’t dominating her and pushing her around.

“You know he’s going back to jail, don’t you?” Alexa asked.

Linda slumped even more than she had been before and gave a little nod.

“You’re in big trouble too. It’s illegal to hide someone who has skipped out on their parole. And then there’s the pot.”

Linda didn’t say anything.

“You working?” Alexa asked.

“I bag groceries at Albertsons.”

“Full time?”

“Thirty hours a week.”

“So no benefits and barely enough money to live on. Then Nathaniel blows into town and wants to party it up.”

"He's good to me."

"He's gotten you in a lot of trouble." Alexa looked at Linda's car, which had obviously not been used for a long time. "How did he get down here?"

"Greyhound."

"He doesn't have a vehicle of his own?"

"No. Nat don't have the money."

"Whose pot is it?"

Linda didn't reply.

"Now Ms. White, I can arrest you on those two charges I mentioned. You might not do time but you'll probably lose your job. Then you'll be in even bigger trouble financially than you are now. I don't want to do that. Nathaniel is going to jail regardless."

"What for?" Linda bawled, tears welling up in her eyes.

Jesus.

Alexa had a flash of this girl's childhood. Bad parents. A house filled with drama. No education. No nurturing.

In other words, a childhood just like Stacy Carpenter's until Alexa had taken her under her wing.

And Linda had grown up to be a perpetual victim, easy prey for any dominating man.

She could not let that happen to Stacy.

Alexa gathered her patience and explained. "He skipped out on two parole meetings and then assaulted me." Alexa rubbed her jaw. It still hurt. "Violating parole is enough to send him back inside. Add the assault charge and he's going to serve at least a couple more years."

Linda started sniffling.

"It's not your fault," Alexa said, much as she said to Stacy over and over again. "He messed up and it's his responsibility."

Linda didn't reply, so Alexa continued.

"Now I don't want you to get into trouble for his sake, so I'd like you to help me out, all right?"

"All right," Linda said in a quiet voice.

"Good, this will help me a lot. And it will help you. Has Nat been here the whole two weeks?"

"Yeah. We just been hanging out."

"What does he do when you're at work?"

"Smoke weed and watch TV mostly."

"Has he seen anyone?"

“He don’t know no one in Marana except me. Said he wanted to keep his head down. Said too many people bugging him in Phoenix. His parole officer was giving him trouble and some of his old buddies was getting into fights with him and stuff. Wanted to come down here and clear his head.”

Clear his head by smoking weed and living off someone below the poverty line.

“So he hasn’t seen anyone down here?”

“No. Just me. We went to the bars a couple of times, and he talked with people there, but didn’t make no friends.”

“How long are your shifts?”

“Six hours.”

“What shift?”

“Whatever they give me. Sometimes the day, sometimes the night.”

“And when does Albertsons close?”

“Eleven.”

Alexa thought a moment. Six hours was enough time for Nathaniel to drive to Benson or Phoenix, commit the murders, and get back before Linda got off her shift. But given that the killer scoped out both neighborhoods thoroughly before breaking into the judges’ houses, there would have had to be at least two trips.

Then there was the problem of Nathaniel not having a known vehicle.

More likely Linda was telling the truth. Alexa had seen it with people skipping their parole. Countless times. Chafing under the lack of freedom, the con would run off to another town, usually with a woman, and think all their problems and obligations would magically disappear.

She and Stuart had to check on some things. Search the apartment thoroughly and grill Nathaniel, but Alexa didn’t hold out much hope.

The killer they were hunting was cold and calculating, good at covering his tracks. This thug was just an idiot. He had called attention to himself by skipping parole and Alexa didn’t think the killer would do that. Also, he had acted rashly, making noise by trying to get out a window when he could have just hidden, and then attacking an officer.

It looked like Nathaniel White wasn’t their man.

And that meant they were back at square one.

The killer was still out there, perhaps planning his next attack.

CHAPTER TWELVE

Kurt Billings was celebrating. He had, once again, nailed some lowlife and put her in jail.

It had been ridiculously easy. Marylin Smith turned out to be a total pushover.

Billings raised his martini glass to toast himself as he sat in the loud, laughing circle of other lawyers at the Executive Lounge, the most expensive piano bar in Phoenix. He took a long sip, settled into the comfortable leather chair, and smiled as he thought of how he had brought his case to a guilty verdict.

"You should have seen her," Billings said to the man next to him, a criminal lawyer and the most junior member of the group. "As soon as she got on the stand I knew I had her. Nervous as hell. The case against her husband was open and shut. The cops busted into his motel room and found him in the bathroom in the act of making meth. So all I had to do was link the two."

The criminal lawyer nodded and smiled encouragingly. The guy was climbing the ladder in Phoenix's legal community and was obviously impressed by the state prosecutor's brilliance, and hoping to forge a good professional connection. Billings went on.

"The defense was putting on this clueless, innocent wife act. Clueless I can believe. She was as dumb as they come. But innocent? Hell, no. Problem was, I had to convince the jury of that."

"And how did you do that?" the lawyer asked, half paying attention to another conversation in the circle.

"Well, I'll tell you. The public defender, Zimmerman, got her all dressed up to play the part. Flowery white shirt and a big cross around her neck. Whole nine yards. Made a good impression on the jury. Zimmerman is a slippery bastard, you got to take care when facing him, but he didn't have much to work with this time. You see, what he didn't know because the police didn't tell him, was that they had found a small amount of marijuana in her home."

The lawyer's brow furrowed. "They're supposed to inform the defense of—"

"Get real, buddy. This isn't the Boy Scouts. The cops knew she was guilty and gave me a helping hand. If Zimmerman didn't know, that's Marylin Smith's fault. Dumb chick had her head in the sand, thinking if she just kept quiet about everything, it would all go away. Ha! So I started cross-examining her. Asked her if she's ever taken drugs, if her husband's taken drugs. And she answered no, no, no. Still the innocent wife role. Manages to act pretty convincing. Zimmerman got his little dog trained well. Then I sprung it on them. I stroll over to the exhibits table, where I'd gotten the officers of the court to keep the bag of marijuana in a manila envelope so Zimmerman wouldn't see it."

"Smart move, I guess," the lawyer said, glancing over at the other conversation.

Billings put his hand roughly on the guy's arm to get his attention. Some of his martini sloshed on the floor. He drained the rest.

"Now listen. Here's where it gets good. I stroll on over to the exhibits table and say, 'Mrs. Smith, you say you never take drugs; then why did you have this in your bedside table?' And I pull out the bag of weed and dangle it in front of her. Oh, God, you should have seen her face!"

"She should have known they'd have found it," the lawyer said. Even through an alcoholic haze, Billings could tell he was more interested now. The state prosecutor bathed in his admiration.

"Boys Scouts, buddy. Boy Scouts!" Billings had gotten loud enough that he was turning heads. So what? A man's got the right to cut loose once in a while. And they should all hear how he nailed Marylin Smith. "So this chick gets all flustered, says it isn't hers, that she didn't smoke pot. 'But it was in your bedside table, Mrs. Smith. You expect the jury to believe it just snuck in there?' She turned red, started muttering, no one could make out a word she said. Perfect. Then I got all fire and brimstone, making the connection the jurors had already made in their mind. 'Mrs. Smith! You say you are a law abiding citizen, that you had no knowledge and nothing to do with your husband's drug production. So please explain why you have drugs in your bedside table?'"

Billings got rewarded with a grin from the junior attorney. "That's a tough question to answer. Sounds like you nailed her."

"Oh sure, the rest was easy. I had her so off the rails I talked circles around her. Caught her in all sorts of contradictions. Made her out to the jury as a pathological liar. Zimmerman didn't have a chance. I almost felt sorry for the schmuck."

The lawyer shook his head in wonder. "I can't believe the defendant didn't tell her attorney about the pot. What an idiot."

"She was an idiot, but not in the way you think," Billings said triumphantly.

"What do you mean?"

"It was in her husband's bedside table, not hers."

The layer blinked. "But you said it was in her bedside table."

Billings shrugged. "They were husband and wife. They owned everything together. So it was just as much her bedside table as it was his, even if it was on his side of the bed."

"But that's—"

Billings cackled. "I blindsided her so bad she didn't even think to mention that! It was a risk, sure, and with a smarter defendant it wouldn't have worked. But I saw she was nervous as hell when she took the stand. You got to remember that this woman had just lost her husband and most of her money. She was a wreck. Then I pummel her with questions, soften her up before popping the big surprise. The jury only retired for an hour. Found her guilty. I can't wait until sentencing. I bet she'll get ten years."

The junior attorney frowned. "Now wait a minute. There were several irregularities—"

Billings waved his objections away. "Law of the jungle. I knew she was guilty, so I had every right—no, an obligation—to put her behind bars. Her life is over and she deserves to rot. She was a useless excuse for humanity anyway."

Billings put down his empty glass, briefly considered ordering another, then saw the two clocks on the nearby wall. Wait, one clock. And it showed it was just past midnight. He had to get up early. Another twelve-hour grind. Damn.

He giggled. The look on that idiot woman's face when the jury declared "guilty." That was worth all the long hours.

"Well, got to go," he stood, steadied himself, tried to slap the young lawyer on the back and ended up hitting him upside the head. "Sorry. Missed."

He chuckled and wove his way to the door. He had paid, right? Didn't matter. He could keep a tab here. All the staff loved him.

Admired him for keeping the city safe. He was the state's best prosecutor.

"State's best prosecutor!" he bellowed, raising his fists in the air. Somebody whooped. Or laughed. No, definitely whooped. They loved him here.

He got to the door and out into the warm Phoenix night. For a moment he stood on the sidewalk. Downtown had grown quiet. Music thudded from a nightclub down the street. A taxi drove by. Other than that, all was silent. No one on the streets.

The state's best prosecutor made his way to the parking lot around the block, singing as he went, the sidewalk rocking like a ship at sea. Nothing he couldn't handle. He'd be all right. A bump? Nah. Not when he had to drive. He was a responsible citizen.

He passed no one. The parking lot was still about a third full, mostly by people at the Executive Lounge and that nightclub. No one was working right now unless they were a bartender. All the office buildings were dark save for a few lights on for the janitors and night watchmen.

He angled across the street toward the parking lot, only realizing after he made it to the other side that he hadn't looked for cars. Oh well. His Lexus was up ahead. He got out his keys, fumbled and dropped them, and bent over to grab them.

That nearly toppled him over. OK. Maybe he did need a bump. Too many martinis had made him clumsy and sleepy. A line would help. Just a little one. Just to clear his head.

He stood, head spinning, let out a belch, and clicked the button on his key chain. The car bleeped, the lights flashed, and the doors unlocked.

Getting inside and closing the door, he fumbled around until he found the Altoids box inside his jacket pocket. Good thing he had the foresight to bring it with him tonight. Moving slowly and deliberately so he didn't drop any of the precious powder, he set up his gear on the dashboard. He had no fear of cops. The door was closed, the windows tinted, and everyone knew he was an upstanding citizen.

Cutting the coke calmed him for some reason, made him sober up a little. It was a ritual that cleared his head. Some people resorted to prayer. He cut lines. That made him giggle and he nearly knocked all the gear off his dashboard.

He steadied himself and got back to work. Once he had made himself a moderately sized line, just enough to level him out and get him home, he rolled up the hundred dollar bill into a nice tight roll, stuck it in his nose and leaned over the line.

Like most drunks, Kurt Billings was drunker than he thought. So drunk that he did not notice the shadowy figure move up to the side of his car. His mind, befuddled by alcohol and anticipating a new high, didn't register the man's presence until the door opened and a strong hand hit him on the back of the head.

Billings cried out as the rolled-up bill jammed deep into his nostril. He drew back on the seat, feeling blood gush from his nose.

"It was an accident!" he cried. "I meant to slap you on the back."

But it wasn't the young lawyer he saw in front of him. No, it was someone very different.

Billings experienced a moment of clarity.

"Oh my God, it's you!"

The knife came down. Billings felt a searing pain as it plunged deep in his chest. Then it came down again, and again. He moaned, unable to resist as the tempo increased, the hard length of razor sharp steel ravaging his flesh.

All he could do was make an incoherent plea for mercy that he knew this man would never give.

CHAPTER THIRTEEN

As Alexa had expected, and dreaded, everything checked out with Nathaniel White. They could find no evidence he had been in Benson or Phoenix at the time of the murders, and he firmly maintained his innocence. The fact that he had no transportation, and no knife or bloody materials were found in his possession, made him a poor suspect.

At least he was behind bars. He deserved to be there anyway.

But that didn't help Alexa and Stuart. They were still stuck with the double murder of two longtime judges.

Processing White had taken long enough that they had grabbed a bite to eat in a local Village Inn and gotten rooms at the Motel 6. It was too late to drive back to Phoenix when they didn't know where this case would next lead them.

Alexa lay on her bed, tired but not sleepy. The late edition news was playing in the background.

"Still no suspects in the murders of two Arizona judges. Police say they are following a number of leads and hope to bring in a suspect within the next day or two. The—"

Alexa switched off the TV in disgust. Whoever had told the press that should be fired. No way would they crack this case in the next couple of days. You didn't just go from having no strong evidence or leads to pulling the guilty party out of a hat.

But that wouldn't stop them from feeling constant pressure to do so.

She slumped back in bed, knowing she couldn't sleep. Thornton's mocking applause kept echoing in her memory. And his revelation that Drake had become a prison guru confirmed her worst fears. She had hoped that getting caught a second time might have taken off some of his shine. It looked like these convicts didn't care. Arresting him had only turned him into a martyr.

God, she missed Robert Powers. He would have said something to make her feel better. He had always been good at that.

Thinking about Robert made her think about his journal. She hadn't had the guts to open it, although she had brought it along on the trip.

Could she deal with another emotional blow today? Maybe she should. Even though it would hurt to read anything by him, it would feel like he was still there a bit, no matter what he wrote.

Rummaging through her overnight bag, she pulled out the leather-bound volume. For a moment she sat on the edge of the bed, running her hand along the smooth leather. It took her a moment to summon the courage to open it to the first page.

At the top of the page was a date from two years before Alexa had joined the U.S. Marshals Service. She had been in the East, working for the FBI, and slowly but surely cracking up. Robert had just been a family friend, not very well known to her but one of those people who had always been around. He and her uncle Frank, who owned a ranch a few miles from her father's, had gone to school together. They had been inseparable for decades, and poor Uncle Frank was flattened by his loss.

So Robert Powers had known but had not particularly gotten along with Alexa's father. Not many people did get along with the prickly, loudmouthed, and judgmental rancher.

There had been respect on both sides, though. She knew that. Alexa's father had always taken care of his family and helped his community. If someone's barn burned in a fire or animals got hit by disease, old Victor Chase would tromp on over to the neighbor and help out. And it didn't matter if Victor Chase was always complaining about the fellow; he'd be there, ready to help. No money would ever change hands—in the rugged morality of the ranching country that would be an insult—just hours and hours of backbreaking toil with nothing expected in return except a homecooked lunch and a couple of beers on the porch when the day's work was done.

It was hard not to respect a man like that, even if you didn't like him.

On the other side, Victor Chase had a grudging respect for U.S. Marshal Robert Powers. He was a lawman, which was a plus, but one who worked at a federal agency, which was a major minus. At least he wasn't one of those "meddling commie bureaucrats" like in the Bureau of Land Management, the Department of Agriculture, or (lowest of the low) the Environmental Protection Agency. And he caught criminals, or "lowlifes," as Alexa's father always called them.

So Robert would not be unwelcome on the ranch on the occasions when Uncle Frank came over, or if there was a local case and Robert wanted to ask Alexa's father and brothers if they had seen or heard anything. They always tried to help. Catching "lowlifes" was about the only thing Victor Chase would do to help the government.

Alexa closed the journal and ran her palm against the smooth, aromatic leather again. Robert Powers had started out as a sort of uncle figure. When she had come back from the East shattered after the Jersey Devil case, he had become a friend. Later, after getting her squared away and ready for the U.S. Marshals Service, he had become a mentor and a partner.

The first feeling had never truly gone away. Alexa felt like she had lost family.

She realized she had closed the book again. She forced herself to reopen it.

Below the date, in Robert's handwriting, the first line said,

"I nearly got killed today."

Alexa blinked. She hadn't heard this story. Most lawmen bragged about things like that, or at least used them as cautionary tales for younger, less experienced, officers.

She read more.

"Cornered that pot dealer we've been chasing all this time. We got a tipoff that he'd be at a trailer on mile 30 of State Route 260. Sure enough, there he was, with several duffel bags that almost knocked me over the pot smell was so strong. How anyone can smoke something that smells like that I'll never know—"

Alexa chuckled, then wiped a tear from her eye. It was almost like his voice was coming through the page. Robert hadn't disapproved of drugs so much as he had been baffled by them. *They all look sleepy and stupid. If I want to be like that, I'll skip my morning coffee.*

She read on.

"—but this guy wasn't smoking. Most of the big dealers never do. They know what this crap does to a person."

Alexa raised an eyebrow. Robert never swore out loud, not even with a word that mild. Interesting that he'd do it in a journal.

"So we approached the trailer, me from the front and Marshal Herrero from the rear. The perp came out shooting. Had a .357 Magnum. Jesus Christ the thing looked like a howitzer. Before I could even tell him to drop it and put his hands up he took a shot at me from ten yards. Maybe even less. The mind plays tricks in situations like that. It seemed like he was right in my face, that the gunshot was louder than a thunderclap.

"I dodged just at the last moment and actually felt the heat of the bullet as it passed by my head. I'm not sure if that was my imagination or not.

"After that I did the only thing I could do. I plugged him. A single shot straight through the body, hoping the bullet didn't pass through him, continue on through the thin metal of the trailer wall, and hit Marshal Herrero. I've heard of things like that happening.

"I got him straight through the heart. I wasn't aiming for it. I didn't have time to make anything more than a snapshot for the torso area. If I had aimed, he would have gotten a second shot off and I wouldn't have been so lucky that time.

"He dropped on the floor and didn't move. At first I didn't realize I'd killed him. I approached, Marshal Herrero coming around to the front of the trailer and assisting me. That guy sure can run fast when he needs to. I kicked the pistol away, checked the trailer for other suspects, then tried to give medical assistance.

"It soon became obvious that he was past saving. Once we secured the area and radioed in a report, Marshal Herrero turned to say something to me and his jaw just dropped.

"'What?' I asked.

"He only pointed to my head, then pointed to the little mirror above the trailer's sink. I went to look.

"The bullet had ploughed a furrow in my sideburn. We had just been joking that I needed a haircut, because my sideburns, which always seem to grow faster than the rest of the hair on my head, were puffing out a bit. Not much, like half an inch, but just enough that you could see a little half circle the size of a .357 Magnum bullet. It had missed my skin by a couple of millimeters. The hair was all singed.

"It's hard to describe the feelings that went through me as I stood and stared into that mirror. Shock, for one. No relief. The relief didn't strike me until later, at the same time as the fear. At the moment all I felt was this numbing awareness of how close I had come, and a smug satisfaction that I had taken the perp out.

"Yeah, I was glad I had killed somebody. I remember I looked down at the body, with all that blood all over the wall and floor, and felt like kicking him. I probably would have if Marshal Herrero hadn't been there. I felt so much contempt, so much superiority that I had lived and he hadn't. Odd. I didn't feel any moral superiority, that I was a Marshal, and he was a drug dealer who peddled dope and had probably killed lots of people. Morals played no part in it. I only felt like an animal who met with another wild beast in the wilderness, fought, and came out on top. It was a hell of a feeling. A better high than anything in those stinking duffel bags could give. Almost sexual.

"Well, like I said, the relief and fear came later. After we got backup, after they had taken my report and photographed the scene and the local P.D. had taken over. Then we drove off to go back to the office. Marshal Herrero offered to drive. He must have seen the state I was in and known that if I had gotten behind the wheel I'd have made it all of about two miles before going off the road and taking out a saguaro.

"I think it was the lack of anything to do that made it come on me. I was just sitting there, Marshal Herrero saying something reassuring that completely passed through my head without me hearing the words, when I suddenly got a trembling fit. And I do mean a fit. An all over shaking like I was an epileptic or something. Embarrassing as hell.

"Embarrassing? That's not fair to Marshal Herrero. No need to be embarrassed in front of that guy. He'd been around. He'd seen it all before. He just slowly and calmly started talking about a time when a guy came at him with a knife in an enclosed apartment. He had busted a crack house and this guy came right at him in a room full of people. Marshal Herrero couldn't fire without maybe hitting one of the other crackheads, so he had to take him down with self-defense techniques. Those flips and holds work pretty good, but you sure don't want to try them on some drug-crazed maniac wielding a Bowie knife.

"He talked about how his uniform got slashed but the blade didn't reach skin, and how once he got the guy cuffed he got all scared and shaky just like I was now.

"Poor guy. I know he was trying to be helpful but he only made me feel worse. Because right when he said it I realized that I wasn't feeling all sick and shaky because I had nearly gotten killed. I reacted like that because of the sick, triumphant feeling in my gut at having killed another man who had tried to kill me. And I knew, deep down, that even if he hadn't gone for me, I would have felt the same about killing him.

"There's a darkness in all our hearts. As officers of the law we pretend we're above the people who give in to it, but we're not really.

No, we're just the same as they are. The only difference is that we manage to control it. Most of the time.

"And deny it. All of the time."

Alexa stared at the page, letting out a long, slow breath.

"So he felt it too," she murmured.

It seemed unbelievable. He had always been so confident, so level-headed, so professional. He had never beaten down a suspect like Alexa had on the last case.

Or had he?

Alexa flipped through the journal. There had to be at least a hundred pages of writing, with dates going up to just a couple of months before he got killed.

She felt tempted to scan through the pages for her name, or go to the date when she had first partnered up with him.

No. It would be better to read it from start to finish. See how he had progressed as a lawman. Because Alexa, despite having several years of experience in the FBI, was still relatively new in the U.S. Marshals Service. She was only a deputy marshal, for example, and Drake Logan had been her only really big case.

Now she was on her second one, fighting that same darkness that Robert Powers had also fought.

But he had never let it show. He had been a professional right to the very end.

That's what I need to do.

Alexa nodded, put the journal carefully back in her suitcase, and got ready for bed.

Her phone rang. Marshal Hernandez. He never called this late unless something big was going down.

Alexa answered. "Hello?"

"Deputy Marshal Chase, sorry to wake you."

"Actually, sir, I wasn't in bed yet."

"Good. There's been another murder."

Alexa perked up. "Where?"

"A state prosecutor in Phoenix named Kurt Billings was murdered just an hour ago. Multiple stab wounds. It looks like our man."

"We'll get right up there."

"No need. The police and CSI are going to be busy most of the night. Come up first thing in the morning."

"It would be better if we saw the scene."

"The Phoenix homicide squad is perfectly capable. You know that. They can handle it and give you a complete report in the morning."

"But—"

"You'll be sharper if you have some sleep, Deputy Marshal Chase."

That came out as an order. Alexa bit her lip, stopping herself from saying anything. She had gotten worn out on the manhunt for Drake Logan, close to the breaking point. It must have been obvious to everyone, especially someone as experienced, and as caring, as her boss.

He didn't want her to get worn out on this one.

He probably didn't even want her on this one. What had he said when she had started her two-week personal break? *Take as much time as you need to. If you need more than two weeks, just ask.*

Had that been more of a hint than an offer? Did he think she wasn't ready to work?

All these thoughts and doubts flashed through her mind in an instant, and her boss heard only the briefest of pauses as she answered, "Yes, sir. We'll be up there first thing. I'll fill in Agent Barrett."

"Thank you. Get some rest."

As soon as he hung up, she dialed Stuart.

"Erm?" came a sleepy voice on the other end of the line.

"You awake enough to drive a hundred down the freeway?" Alexa asked.

"Sure. Why? Has there been another murder?"

Alexa blinked. He had gone from asleep to alert in less than two seconds.

"Yes there has."

"I'll meet you at the car in five."

Alexa got to the car in four. Stuart was already waiting.

CHAPTER FOURTEEN

Alexa fumed. Despite Stuart nearly giving her a heart attack with his driving, the murder scene had been mostly cleansed by the time they got up there.

While the car was still there, and the entire parking lot sealed off with police tape, the body had been taken. Once again she had to rely on police photos.

At least they had already printed out a preliminary report, knowing she and Stuart were coming. Marshal Hernandez was right. With Phoenix's high murder rate, the homicide squad was efficient and all too experienced.

She and Stuart stood next to the Lexus with the tinted windows. The driver's side door hung open. The front seats and floor were soaked with dried blood. Splashes of it marked the inside windows. Another furious stabbing. On the pavement next to the open door was a dried patch of blood and a couple of bloody partial footprints from where the perp had stepped into the puddle with the front half of their shoe and then tried to wipe it away on the pavement. Their first solid clue.

But was this their man? The timing and method of murder were the same, but the killing had taken place outside, not at the victim's home. If this was the same killer, why the change?

There were only three policemen standing at the crime scene, posted there to keep anyone from interfering with it. They hadn't been the officers who took the call the night before. CSI was due back any minute to recheck the parking lot. The team had collected the body and escorted it to the morgue, and would now come back to finish up. So at the moment, she and Stuart were left without anyone who had actually been there.

Anger bubbled up inside her. Marshal Hernandez wanted her to wait until morning. She would have really missed everything then. He should have more faith in her.

Then a sudden worry came to her mind. What if he had heard about her visit to the Jersey Devil? While it was perfectly legal for her to visit a convict in prison, he would think that didn't look good for her mental state.

If he only knew how bad it was.

Focus. You need to focus if you want to crack this case and prove to him you're still capable.

You need to do that to prove it to yourself.

"Looks like this whole area is well covered with security cameras," Alexa said. "We should get some images of our killer."

"The cops will be getting those first thing. It's at the top of the to do list here. Wish they hadn't moved the body, but with someone that important I'm not surprised. Hey, look at this." Stuart flipped to another page of the initial report and pointed at one of the photographs, showing State Prosecutor Kurt Billings lying twisted and bloody across his front seat.

His finger indicated a slightly open mouth filled with blood. The lower lip was cut deeply.

"Looks like he forked Billings's tongue," Alexa said. "He cut the lip too. He didn't do that in the previous two. I bet it was because of the exposed murder site. He felt nervous and got in too much of a hurry."

Stuart nodded, then tapped a small, rolled up paper crunched into one nostril.

"The report says this is a hundred dollar bill. They found some cocaine in the car. I bet when toxicology runs their tests we'll see that Billings had been using."

"Killed in the act of taking illegal drugs. I wonder if that's part of the motive. Punishing someone who was sending people to jail for something they did themselves."

"Maybe. Maybe it's just incidental, though. Judges Warburton and Rodriguez seem to have been clean. I called the FBI and our agency wasn't investigating them for anything."

Alexa looked around the parking lot, hoping the empty stretch of concrete and the surrounding glass and steel high rises might give her an answer. On the street opposite was a line of TV vans, already putting up their satellite hookups. One male reporter had already positioned himself next to the police line, where a cop had gone to make sure no one jumped it, and was preparing to speak into a camera his crew had set up.

Alexa's eye ran along the line of vans until she saw, to her dismay but not surprise, the red and white logo of Action News. Her brother

Wayne's wife, Melanie, worked as a reporter for Action News. Alexa couldn't see her in the crowd and hoped someone else had come to report on this story. While Alexa had made it clear on many occasions that Melanie could not use her as a source, that hadn't stopped the reporter from trying.

A much more welcome sight was the CSI lab truck pulling up. Cameras rushed to film it, and several reporters hurried over, wielding their microphones and asking questions to the crew even before they made it out of the van.

Alexa's heart sunk when she saw Melanie among them. She turned away and studied the crime scene again. She didn't see any of the telltale chalk circles the CSI team left when they found items that might be clues. Whoever this killer was, he was careful to leave a minimum of evidence.

So once again, why kill someone in an open parking lot with cameras? Desperation? An escalation of emotion? If the latter, he might kill again, and soon.

On the other hand, it also might make him slip up. They were drawing closer to the killer.

Stuart's face looking over her shoulder and taking on a sudden male interest told her who was leading the CSI team.

She turned to see Annette Guevara approaching at the head of three male assistants.

Alexa had no idea what the general population's stereotype of a CSI investigator was. Probably a slightly creepy older man with thick glasses and unfashionable clothes.

Annette Guevara certainly did not fit that description. A petite Mexican-American who looked ten years younger than her thirty-two, she had long brown hair, an oval face, and eyes that wouldn't have looked out of place on Bambi. It was hard to remember that this beautiful, childlike woman had already earned a Ph.D. in biology, several commendations from the city, and the reputation of being the best criminal investigator in the entire state.

It was doubly hard for men to do so.

"Hi!" Stuart said, obviously delighted. Alexa resisted the urge to jab an elbow in his ribs.

"Hello," Annette's eyes flicked over Stuart, who tensed a little at the scrutiny. "FBI?"

"Um, yes. Special Agent Stuart Barrett."

"What happened to your usual suit?"

Stuart blinked. "I beg your pardon?"

"You're wearing your backup suit. I can tell because it's been in a suitcase and not been properly pressed afterwards. Your first suit, which certainly was properly pressed given your overall tidy appearance, must have gotten dirty and you had to quickly replace it with this one. You tackled someone in a sandy area. A wash, perhaps?"

The other members of the CSI snickered. So did Alexa. She'd seen Annette pull this before.

"Uhhh … "

Not one of your more intelligent replies, Stuart.

Annette pointed to his fingernails. "You washed your hands well enough, but there are a trace amounts of sand under your nails. Probably had to hurry in the bathroom to get out here this soon. I bet you got your man, though. College football and a stint in the armed forces makes you fitter than most criminals."

"Who are you?" Stuart managed to say. "Mrs. Sherlock Holmes?"

"No. My name is Annette Guevara." She gave him a sweet smile. "*Miss* Annette Guevara."

"Oh." Stuart got himself together. "So what can you tell us, Miss Guevara?"

"Or Doctor Guevara, if you like."

"Um. Right."

Alexa smiled. Annette liked to bowl over male officers with a display of her brilliance. It stopped most of the flirting and replaced it with respect. Annette usually didn't reduce the effect with flirtation of her own. That "Miss" bit was not like her. Nor was the admiring look she gave Alexa's partner.

Could we get to the murder now? Alexa just managed not to say that out loud.

Luckily, that appreciative look didn't last long. The CSI official turned to her.

"Hi, Alexa! Collaborating with the FBI now, eh? Well, to answer your cute partner's question, we don't have much yet although the labs are still working on some stuff. Near as I can make out, the victim was snorting some coke on the dashboard of his car here when the perp opened the door, slammed his face down on the dash, which jammed the hundred dollar bill he was using right up into his sinuses, and then slashed and stabbed the guy to death. Once he was down, the perp slit his tongue, cutting the lower lip as he did so. Righthanded, strong, enraged. Not too tall considering the angle of the cut wounds while taking into account that he had to be hunched halfway inside the vehicle. So you're looking for a shorter male, maybe about the height of Agent Barrett here. So short but not unattractively short. Still looking like a man should."

Stuart made a little strangling sound. Doctor (or Miss) Guevara went on.

"We dusted for prints, of course, and we already got those back. None but the victim's. The perp wore gloves. The big clue is these shoe prints. As you can see, he stepped in a little puddle of blood and got the front half of his right sneaker—size ten and a half, big shoes for a shorter man—stained with blood. He wiped it all around to try and get rid of it, but he still left enough of a print to identify the shoes as Adidas Performance Bounce, this year's edition. They're running shoes with a mesh top for better breathability. Considering the splash, some blood might have soaked through to his sock. Certainly his pants and shirt would have been covered in it. As you can see from this faint blood print here, made after he wiped his foot and too faint for him to have seen at night under streetlight, he moved away and crouched, then repositioned his foot again. Most likely he was doing a quick change out of his bloody clothes, putting them into a duffel bag or something before making his way off downtown."

No, Alexa didn't see that, but she trusted Annette's expertise.

"Thanks, Annette. Anything more for us?"

"Not yet. I'll call you when I get anything. Homicide told me to tell you they're pulling the camera footage now, so come on down to the station in a bit and they'll show it to you. In the meantime, Billings's office address is in the preliminary report your partner has in his hand." Stuart stared at it. It was in a plain manila folder. Closed. "His secretary and paralegal have been called in. So you might want to go question them while you wait."

"Um, all right." Talking with Annette always made her feel like standing in the middle of a dust devil, being pulled around and around faster than she could think.

"Thank you very much for your help, Miss, er, Doctor Guevara," Stuart put in.

"You're welcome. And no, it wouldn't be stereotyping to ask me out for Mexican food. I'm free after nine on weeknights and anytime on weekends. Coming from back East I bet you've never had any of the real stuff. One rule, don't ask if I'm related to Che. He was a scumbag. Put Cuban gays in prison camps. Yes, I'm bisexual. No, that's not a threat to you."

"Right. So, um, can I have your number?"

"Find it yourself, investigator. Now run along. Alexa is a workaholic and all this standing around is making her antsy." She turned to her assistants. "Come on, guys, let's get to work."

Having been dismissed, Alexa and Stuart walked away.

"Wow," Stuart whispered.

Alexa gave him an annoyed glance. "Find the address for Billings's office and let's go. I'm sure the police have called his coworkers in to be interviewed. But let's go out that way."

She pointed to the side of the parking lot opposite of where the news crews were stationed. The last thing she needed right now was having to deal with her sister-in-law.

But shaking family isn't so easy, and they hadn't made it half a block before the Action News van shrieked to a halt right next to them.

CHAPTER FIFTEEN

Melanie jumped out and hurried over to Alexa. A cameraman hustled close behind.

Alexa rounded on her. "Melanie, what have I told you about trying to interview me? It's conflict of interest and you can get me in trouble."

Melanie, a tall, willowy blonde wearing the heavy makeup needed for television, ignored what Alexa said, the same as she always had.

"Is it true you've been assigned to the Billings murder?"

"Yes, but I can't comment on it," Alexa said, still walking. Stuart managed to get between the cameraman and her, blocking his shot.

"Is this case related to the recent murders of Judges Warburton and Rodriguez?"

"No comment."

Alexa picked up the pace. The camera dodged back and forth, trying to get her in the frame, but Stuart showed his football skills and managed to fill up the shot with the back of his black suit. Not very interesting to television viewers. And if something isn't visually interesting, Alexa knew, it wouldn't make it on the news.

"Please, Alexa, this is an important case."

"Which is why I'm not going to prejudice it by speaking to you." Why her reserved, country-boy brother Wayne ever married someone like this was beyond Alexa's understanding.

"Alexa, come on. I just—"

"No comment."

Melanie turned to Stuart. So did the cameraman. Stuart put his hand on the lens.

"And what's your role in this investigation?" Melanie asked.

"No comment."

"The public has a right to know."

"No comment."

They had made it to Billings's office building. The security guard, a hefty black man who looked like he had played football with Stuart in college, let them in and then blocked the door to the two reporters.

Melanie demanded to be let in. The security guard, no doubt sensing there was no reasoning with this woman, didn't bother to reply.

"Friend of yours?" Stuart asked as they went up the elevator.

"Sister-in-law," Alexa grumbled.

Stuart didn't reply. Smart man.

The elevator opened and greeting them was another familiar face from Phoenix law enforcement, Homicide Detective John Rebstock.

Rebstock couldn't have been more different than Guevara. He was a mountain of a man. Standing six-five and weighing at least three hundred pounds, he had a florid face and red nose that told of a career of heavy drinking. He wore a wrinkled, light tan suit and smelled of cigarettes and cheap aftershave.

He did not make a good impression, but Alexa knew he was almost as good at his job as Guevara was at hers. The only difference was that he was only highly intelligent, rather than a certified genius.

"Hey, Alexa. Heard you were coming. And this must be Special Agent Barrett. Rebstock. Homicide."

"Pleased to meet you," Stuart shook his hand.

"I was waiting for you before interviewing the coworkers. I already interviewed the man who found him. A bartender at the Executive Lounge, where Billings was a regular. Billings stayed there partying it up until about midnight before heading out. The bartender said he was pretty drunk. When the bartender went to that same parking lot to get in his car and go home, he recognized Billings's car still there. At first he thought the guy had fallen asleep, but as he got closer he saw the blood, opened up the door, and found the body. I can get him to talk to you if you want."

"That's all right," Alexa said, trusting Rebstock to handle that himself. "Let's go talk to the coworkers."

They walked down the hall past a couple of brass plaques advertising a financial advisor and a tax account and came to a door marked with Billings's name. Rebstock entered without knocking. In the waiting room, sitting stiff and nervous, was an older woman of about sixty and a woman who looked like a recent college graduate.

Neither looked sad. Shocked and nervous, but not sad. Interesting.

Rebstock gestured at them. "This is Hannah Dobbs, Billings's legal assistant, and Geraldine Brooks, his secretary."

There were murmured hellos all around. Then the three officers of the law looked at one another. Who took precedence? It was her and

Stuart's case, but this was Rebstock's turf. To his credit, the homicide detective gave Alexa a little gesture indicating she should take the lead.

Normally she liked to speak to those who knew a victim separately, but since they worked together and had obviously been talking before the officers had entered, she didn't see any point.

"Do either of you know of any threats against Mr. Billings?"

The young paralegal shook her head. Geraldine, the secretary, spoke up.

"There was one man he put away a few years ago—before your time, Hannah—who swore he'd kill him if he ever got out."

Rebstock pulled out a pen and notepad. "What was his name?"

"Donald Paulson. He went in for assault and battery. A violent, vulgar man. That was quite some time ago and I would not be surprised if he was out by now."

Alexa turned to Stuart. "I don't remember that name from our list."

"Neither do I," the FBI man said.

Great, as if the list isn't long enough.

"Anyone else?" Alexa asked.

"There was Armando Lopez. He threatened Mr. Billings for when Mr. Billings got him convicted for drug offenses. That was just two years ago, though, so he might not be out."

Hannah spoke up. "Oh, and there was that guy from Los Cuatro Milpas."

Alexa perked up. That was a Hispanic gang in Phoenix's rough and poor East side.

"Oh yes," Geraldine said. "He was put away for a stabbing."

That got everyone's attention.

"What was his name?" Alexa asked.

"Fernando something," Hannah something. She looked to Geraldine, who put her hand to her chin, trying to remember.

"Fernando Mendoza?" Rebstock asked.

"That's it!" the two women said together.

The homicide cop shook his head. "Can't be him. He was the victim of his own stabbing six months ago. He's dead."

"Can you think of anyone else?" Alexa asked, dreading even more additions to the list.

The two women looked at each other.

"Not anyone else that he convicted."

Odd turn of phrase. "What do you mean by that?"

“Well … ” Hannah blushed, looked at the older woman, who nodded. “Well, he kind of harassed women a lot.” She went on quickly. “He didn’t touch me or anything like that, but he was always dropping hints, like he’d say he knew of a great Japanese restaurant or that he got tickets to the Phoenix Suns. He never directly asked me out on a date, but that’s what he was doing. And he always stared at my chest. Kind of creepy. I started wearing loose sweaters to make him stop. Geraldine had to turn up the air conditioning just so I wouldn’t be too hot.”

“Do you know if he harassed anyone else?” Alexa asked.

Geraldine answered. “Mr. Billings went through three assistants in my time with him, all young graduates and all pretty. He made passes at all of them. I don’t think he ever did anything forceful, but it was unpleasant enough that I know at least two of them left because of it. They told me.”

“Any angry boyfriends?”

“I suppose so. None made any threats.”

Hannah spoke up. “Well, I hate to say this, but my boyfriend said if Mr. Billings ever touched me he’d break both his arms.”

“Did he have problems with other women, such as outside of work?” Alexa asked.

Both women shrugged.

“Outside of work, I didn’t go near him,” Hannah said.

It didn’t matter if they didn’t know. Alexa could guess. A guy who would harass people in the workplace would be twice as bad with people outside of it.

“Can you think of anyone else who might want to harm Kurt Billings?”

The two women said no.

Detective Rebstock inclined his head to indicate they should step out for a minute. Back in the hallway he said, “I spoke with the bartender in the Executive Lounge, and he told me Billings was quite the drinker. Was there regularly, bragging to everyone who’d listen about his record as a state prosecutor. A lot of people didn’t like him. No fights, though.”

Stuart spoke up. “With the booze and the coke, I wonder how good that record was.”

“Spotty,” Rebstock said. “He’s won some and lost some. He hasn’t screwed up too much to lose his job, but his reputation as a prosecutor is not the best. In fact, it’s been declining.”

"Due to increased substance abuse?" Alexa asked.

"That's my guess," the detective said.

Stuart shook his head. "Great. So this guy might have had enemies outside of work," Stuart said. "Angry boyfriends. Rivals who hated him. Maybe a drug connection gone bad. The list could go on and on."

"True enough," Alexa said, "but the other two victims don't seem to have that problem. I'm thinking it's still related to some old case. Now that we have three victims, we should be able to narrow down the overlap between them easily."

Stuart thought for a moment. When he did that, his heavy brow crinkled and he got a bit of a pained look on his face. If Alexa hadn't known him better, she would have thought he looked a bit slow. He was anything but.

"You know, maybe we need to expand our search rather than narrow it down," he said.

"What do you mean?"

"What if it isn't an old case? What if it's a pending case? Or one that is currently in progress? And not necessarily the defendant, but a friend or relation of the defendant."

Alexa thought for a moment. Yes, that could very well be.

Her heart sunk. Yeah, that was certainly a possibility, and that meant they had even more work ahead of them.

The killer seemed further away than ever.

CHAPTER SIXTEEN

Down at the station, Alexa watched as Rebstock showed her and Stuart the security camera footage.

"The cameras are all high up on the buildings," the homicide detective said, fiddling with a desktop computer. "So they're all long shots. The killer took care not to come close to any ATMs or doorway cams."

Scoped out the scene even for this outdoor attack, Alexa thought. *This guy knows what he's doing.*

The video came on. It showed the parking lot in black and white, Billings's vehicle parked almost in the center, with only a few other cars scattered throughout the lot.

The state prosecutor came into view, weaving across the lot, obviously drunk.

After a moment, another figure came into view. It looked like a man, but it was hard to tell because the figure wore a hooded sweatshirt, along with sweatpants, sneakers, and carried a large gym bag. A casual viewer would assume he was coming back from a late-night gym session.

Alexa guessed the height at about five-eight, although it was hard to tell given the angle and distance. A bit stocky. Walked in that ponderous way stocky men do. The figure followed about ten yards behind Billings.

"Look how he keeps directly behind the victim," Stuart said. "In Iraq, locals psyching themselves up for a suicide stabbing would try doing that to us."

"Suicide stabbing?" Alexa asked.

"Not everyone had access to a suicide belt. You had to have connections to the insurgency or one of the Islamist militias to get that. So some people would decide to do it themselves. Tuck a butcher knife under their shirt, follow right behind us, and attack if we weren't paying enough attention. They knew they'd get killed, no way you can take out an entire squad that way, but they hoped to kill or maim at least one of us. Hard to stop a man who wasn't afraid to die."

Alexa shuddered. The things this man had seen. It put her own suffering in perspective. While she had to deal with the worst of humanity on a day-to-day basis, she got to go home to a loving kid and a pair of horses. What did he get to go home to? A barracks full of homesick young men and women who got rockets launched at them in their sleep.

She set that thought aside and studied the footage. The killer, just as Stuart had noted, walked directly behind and about ten yards distant from Billings, who was too drunk to notice him. Many sober men would probably not have noticed him either. A woman would have, but women are more attentive when walking alone at night.

Billings got in the car and closed the door. The killer increased his pace, then slowed, coming up on the back of the car.

Why not rush for the door? Didn't he worry Billings might lock it?

The killer stopped for a moment, then looked around. The deep hood kept his or her features in shadow.

"I checked every camera. No angle gives a view of the face," the homicide detective grumbled.

"Why is he waiting?" Stuart asked. "I don't see anyone passing by."

"Could he know Billings is doing lines?" Alexa suggested. "Maybe he wants to catch him in the act."

"How would he know?" Rebstock asked.

Alexa shrugged. She had no answer to that. His two coworkers didn't seem to know, and considering all the negative things they said about him, you'd think they'd be forthcoming with that information.

Unless they were too intimidated by the presence of three officers. It's one thing to mention sexual harassment, quite another to admit someone was using illegal drugs and you never called the cops.

The killer unzipped the top of his duffle bag and in a single fluid motion drew a large knife, dropped the bag, strode the remaining two steps to the car door, and flung it open.

He or she reached inside and looked like he hit Billings.

That must be the blow to the back of the head.

There was a brief glimpse of Billings's legs as he drew back along the front seats, then the killer bent into the vehicle. They could see the knife hand stabbing and stabbing with quick efficiency.

Alexa's blood ran cold. There was rage there, but also calculation. This was no maniac who had snapped. This person knew exactly what they were doing and went about it with purpose and precision.

A bit of blood spurted out of the car and onto the pavement.

After a few moments, the killer withdrew, gave a quick look around, and closed the car door. As he stepped away from the vehicle, he trod on the puddle of blood. The killer noticed immediately, and wiped the stained shoe repeatedly, purposely smearing the footprint.

"Just like Annette said he would," Stuart whispered. "What a woman."

Rebstock chuckled. "She's roped another one, eh?"

"Quiet, guys," Alexa muttered.

The killer moved over to the gym bag, put the knife inside, then shucked off the sweatpants and hoodie. Underneath were a dark pair of track pants and a dark-colored hooded sweatshirt. He was careful to keep that hood up as he removed the outer one.

He, because he made one little slip. As he pulled the hoodie over his head, the second one pulled up to reveal a slight belly and hair below the navel.

"We got ourselves a guy," Rebstock said just as Alexa was about to point out the same thing.

The killer put the bloody clothes into the gym bag, making the exact same foot movements Annette Guevara had said he had. This didn't surprise Alexa in the least. She had worked with the CSI expert before.

The killer then zipped up the bag and strolled with remarkable calm out of the parking lot and down the street. Rebstock turned off the video.

"Another camera picks him up when he goes around the corner of 6th Street. He goes all the way to Main and turns left before we lost him. Never breaks stride or speeds up. Cool as a cucumber."

"Controlled rage," Alexa murmured.

"Any idea why he didn't go after Billings in his residence like with the other two judges?" Stuart asked.

"We checked his home," the homicide detective said. "He has a penthouse in an exclusive apartment building. Security guard at the front desk twenty-four seven plus security cameras. We're going through the camera footage to try and find some images of our man casing the place. I don't hold out much hope. Our guy is too careful. He probably took one look at the building from down the street and realized it was too risky."

"What about video footage around his workplace?" Alexa asked. "The killer must have watched him for a while to get his routine."

"We're working on that too. In the meantime, we don't have much else."

Alexa looked at her partner. "Looks like we need to sit down and start trawling through the cases again. I like your suggestion about current and scheduled cases. Why don't you do those and I'll keep on the older ones?"

"Will do," Stuart said, rising. "I sure hope we find something quick. I got a feeling this guy isn't done."

* * *

Stuart Barrett had no problem keeping focus as he went through the details of case after case. A state prosecutor had a heavy workload, and he had to check every case, even the ones where the suspect was a woman. Just because the perp was a guy didn't mean a woman wasn't behind it. Several male murderers in recent years had turned out to be working for girlfriends or even mothers.

The focus he had learned from his time in Iraq. Over there, you had to be switched on at all times. What were those guys doing standing at the corner? Had that market cart piled high with vegetables been left alone too long? Is anyone appearing at any window within sight?

He could maintain that sort of attention for hours, although by the end of the day he would always be exhausted.

No time for exhaustion now. They had a killer to catch.

He did have one little distraction, though. That lovely, slim CSI investigator. Wow. Beauty, sass, and genius all rolled into one. Stuart hadn't had a girlfriend in a few months. The demands of his job made it kind of hard to maintain a relationship, and it was difficult meeting people. He didn't like the bar scene and his few experiments with dating apps had been disastrous. But now, just as he moved across the country, he had met a remarkable woman on the job.

The idea of taking her out made him smile.

But enough of that, he told himself. *You don't get any fun until this is over.*

All work and no play make Stuart a dull boy.

Yeah, well, you have to be a dull boy for a while.

At least he was sitting in a cool air conditioned office, away from the searing Arizona summer sun.

And then, just as his stomach began to growl for some lunch, he hit on a serious suspect.

Derek Baxter was a two-time loser standing at the plate ready to make his third strike. He had done two stints in prison for armed robbery. His first case was when he held up a convenience store on the highway near Benson. Judge Rodriguez gave this first offender with a clean record six years, of which he served four for good behavior.

The next offense was a year after he got out of prison, when he held up a liquor store in Phoenix. Judge Warburton gave him ten years. Once again he was released early for good behavior, only serving seven years.

The prison system should have learned its lesson the first time, because only four months after he got out he was charged with another armed robbery, again of a liquor store and again in Phoenix. Judge Warburton would again preside and Billings would represent the prosecution.

Derek Baxter was in serious trouble this time, because Arizona had a three strikes law, meaning that if an offender was convicted three times for certain felonies, he got a mandatory life sentence. Armed robbery was one of those felonies.

The case for the third armed robbery wasn't open and shut, however, so Baxter had been released on bail pending trial. Bail had been set at half a million dollars by a suspicious court, but Baxter had somehow come up with the money.

That set off a big red light in Stuart's head. This guy was a small-time thug with no visible means of income. Where would he get money like that? The details of the bail weren't in this file.

The photo showed a potential match for the guy in the security camera footage. Baxter stood five nine, with short brown hair that would not have shown from the inside of that hood. He had the belly too. More than what appeared in the security camera, but the photo was taken in prison and many inmates lost weight after they got released.

The only thing that didn't really match was Baxter's preferred weapon. In all cases he had used a pistol. That didn't bother Stuart too much. It made sense to use a pistol. A knife doesn't look nearly as intimidating to someone standing behind a counter.

Without a word, Stuart spun his office chair around and launched himself across the room, the little wheels on the chair gliding him across the floor to Alexa's desk.

She chuckled. "You're acting like Stacy."

"Bring her to the office some time. We'll race down the hall."

Stuart grabbed her chair, which also had wheels, and launched them back across the room, stopping in front of his computer.

Alexa laughed, but stopped laughing when she saw what was on the screen.

She read, her face growing serious.

"Good behavior," she said. "He can behave when it suits him. That shows control. You thinking that he wanted to delay his trial by killing the state prosecutor and both judges?"

"The prospect of life in prison might have affected his reasoning. Or maybe he knew he would go down no matter what, so he decided to literally stick it to the man."

"His apartment isn't far," Alexa said, standing up. "Let's go."

CHAPTER SEVENTEEN

Stuart studied the apartment building. It was a cheap two-story affair of concrete in a run-down neighborhood. No standalone houses here, just more concrete apartment complexes and a couple of vacant lots filled with trash. Behind Baxter's apartment complex was a strip mall with a liquor store, a pawn shop, a bail bondsman, and a porn shop. Baxter's string of armed robberies had not brought him prosperity.

And yet he had come up with half a million in bail money.

A couple of tough looking guys sat in lawn chairs in a nearby lot, smoking cigarettes and drinking beer. Stuart wondered if they were drug dealers. He didn't wonder about the guy idling on a nearby corner holding a golf club. "Putting around the green." It meant he dealt pot.

But Stuart wasn't going to go after some small-time dealer. He had a potential killer he needed to visit, one who was almost certainly armed and dangerous.

They got out of the car, which Stuart had parked right in front of the apartment complex. Baxter's place, number 12, looked out onto the street. The blinds were drawn.

"You sure we shouldn't call for backup?" Stuart asked.

"A cop car would attract too much attention," Alexa said.

"Your uniform and my suit don't exactly blend in."

"True enough. But I think we can handle it."

The guy with the golf club spat on the pavement. The two men drinking beer stared at them. One surreptitiously reached into his pocket and flung something behind a nearby cluster of cactus. Stuart was reminded of those kids in the San Pedro Café. He should call them soon, put the scare into them.

They went up the bare concrete steps past cigarette butts and a couple of empty plastic baggies. The door to apartment 11 opened just as they got to the top. A rotund little woman with bloodshot eyes stepped out, took one look at them, and went back in, slamming the door.

They went to Baxter's apartment. Both drew their guns without consulting each other. Given Baxter's history, it was the only sane response.

Standing on either side of the door in case the suspect decided to shoot through it, Stuart reached his hand over and knocked.

"Derek Baxter, this is the FBI and U.S. Marshals Service. We want to talk with you. Open the door and keep your hands in sight."

No response.

Of course there's no response, Stuart grumbled inwardly. *These guys never do as they're told.*

Stuart knocked again. "Last chance, Mr. Baxter."

Still no response.

Stuart raised his eyebrows at Alexa, who inclined her head toward the door.

At least this guy probably doesn't have an IED.

Just then the sharp tang of crystal meth wafted through the air.

Alexa crinkled her nose and looked at Stuart. They nodded to each other.

Crime in progress. Unresponsive suspect. Reasonable suspicion. I get to do what I do best.

Stuart gave the door a swift kick, the cheap wood splintering, the door flying open.

They rushed in, Stuart taking the lead, gun leveled.

They found themselves in a studio apartment, an unmade sofa bed taking up one side. On the opposite side was a cheap card table with a small TV on top. A filthy kitchenette, the sink piled with dirty dishes, took up one corner.

The only other room was the bathroom. The door to it stood open, and he could see a sink and part of the shower. He rushed in, going low around the corner. No one. A huge cockroach scuttled across the tile. It had to be more than an inch long. Stuart curled his lip in disgust. He still wasn't used to Arizona cockroaches.

But there was still that smell of meth …

Stuart moved around the apartment, sniffing until he got to where it smelled the strongest.

The open back window.

"Whoops," Alexa said.

"Shall we bust the downstairs neighbors?"

"We got bigger fish to fry."

"Yeah, but he's gone," Stuart grumbled. "I guess we wait. Maybe he went to … "

His voice trailed off as he noticed a wall calendar by the door. Today's date was circled, along with the words "Winston and Goldberg Legal Services."

"Uh-oh," he muttered, his veins getting doused with ice water. The fourth victim?

Alexa took one look at the calendar and said, "Let's go."

They ran out of the apartment, Alexa getting on her phone. But the time they made it to the car she had already pulled up the law firm's address.

"Give me directions while I drive," Stuart said.

"Straight, then right. Keep on until I tell you."

Stuart peeled out down the street. In the rearview mirror, he saw the two guys in lawn chairs stand up and stroll toward the apartment building. Stuart realized they hadn't secured Baxter's door with a chain or anything. Oh well.

"I'm calling the law firm," Alexa said, punching at her phone.

"Right." Stuart focused on weaving through traffic.

"Busy. No answer." Alexa got on the police radio, calling for backup.

They sped through Phoenix, Stuart blowing two red lights and cutting off several motorists. He had to force himself to concentrate solely on the road and not scan the rooftops for snipers like he had for four long years in Iraq. His pulse pounded and a smile crept across his face.

Damn, I really am addicted to this drama, aren't I? And this time we can even win.

"Phoenix P.D. are sending backup," Alexa said. "Take a right here. I'm calling the law firm again." Pause. "Still no answer!"

"How much further?"

"Just one mile."

Stuart hit the gas, passing an SUV, the driver blaring her horn at him. He noticed Alexa wasn't nagging him about his driving. She never did when the situation was critical. Nice that they were still working together. He hoped it would last.

It won't last if you don't survive your encounter with Derek Baxter. Stay frosty around that guy.

They took the final turn onto a nicer, commercial road as the police radio crackled the location of the nearest responding patrol car, an intersection that meant nothing to Stuart.

"We'll get there two minutes before they do," Alexa said. "It's just up ahead and to the left."

Stuart saw the sign and, cutting across two lanes of traffic, squealed into the parking lot in front of a small office building.

"Jesus!" Alexa cried. "If you want to get killed, leave that to the killer."

"Wimp."

Stuart leapt out of the car. Alexa was right beside him as they rushed into the building's small lobby and, seeing no security on duty, ran up two flights of steps to the law offices.

They came to a quiet, cool hallway, their steps silenced by carpeting. An oak door stood at one end with a sign reading, "Winston and Goldberg Legal Services."

Creeping up to the door, Stuart put his ear to it and listened. The door must have been thick, because the sounds he heard came through muffled.

Not muffled enough for him to miss what was going on. A man was shouting.

"Something's going down," Stuart said. They both drew their guns.

Stuart put his hand on the doorknob, hoping it was unlocked. He probably wouldn't be able to kick this one in on the first try, and he sure as hell didn't want to warn Baxter.

He eased the doorknob a little and found he was in luck. It was unlocked.

A glance at his partner, who nodded. He took a deep breath and, just as another shout came from inside the office, he flung it open.

Stuart and Alexa rushed into the room, guns leveled.

They found themselves in a reception room, but no one sat at the desk. There were two doors at the far wall, one open and one closed. Through the open one they could see a short, grizzled man in grubby jeans and an old t-shirt standing and shouting at someone out of sight.

As the man turned at the sound of the door hitting the wall, Stuart recognized him as Derek Baxter.

"Federal agents. Freeze and put your hands in the air!" he shouted.

Baxter gaped, raising his hands. "What is it this time?"

"Turn around. Put your hands flat on the wall with your legs outspread!" Stuart ordered.

Baxter assumed the position with the speed of a professional with many years of experience.

A voice came from around the corner.

"My name is Martin Goldberg. This is my office. Do I have your permission to come around the corner?"

Sure sounds like a lawyer.

"Are you injured, Mr. Goldberg?"

"No."

"Did he threaten you?"

"No, he was only shouting because he was upset. May I come out now?"

An older man in a suit, with a fringe of gray hair around a bare scalp came into view. He had his hands in the air.

"I need to see some ID," Stuart said, approaching him. Alexa went and handcuffed Baxter.

"I didn't do anything!" Baxter bawled. "I just came to see a lawyer!"

Although he complained, he did not resist. Stuart began to have doubts.

"Why was he shouting?" Stuart demanded.

"He was upset that I didn't hold out much hope for his case."

"Where's your partner? And your secretary?"

"Doing research at court. Can I put my hands down now?"

Stuart looked around the well-appointed office. "Are you taking on his case pro bono?"

"No."

"You think a guy like this can afford you?"

"He's already paid me a retainer."

"In cash?"

"Yes. Can I put my hands down now?"

"Oh, right. Yeah."

The lawyer put his hands down, reached into his pocket, and pulled out some ID.

Alexa searched Baxter, found nothing, and sat him down. Stuart's doubts rose even higher. Alexa cocked her head and studied him for a moment. "We've been to your apartment. Not exactly a penthouse suite. Where did you get the money to hire a lawyer?"

Baxter looked away. "I don't have to tell you anything."

"How about you tell us where you were last night at around midnight?"

"Desert Heat. Why?"

"We're asking the questions," Stuart said. "What's Desert Heat?"

"Freeze!"

Stuart spun around. Two Phoenix police officers stood at the doorway, guns leveled.

"We have this under control," Alexa said.

"Oh, sorry Deputy Marshal," one of the cops said. "You were standing behind this gentleman here," he indicated Stuart. "We didn't see your uniform at first."

"I'm FBI. You need to see my ID?"

"No need. We heard the FBI was called in, and the Deputy Marshal's presence corroborates your story. Who's the other suit?"

"Martin Goldberg, Derek Baxter's attorney," the lawyer said. He had his hands up again.

"Everything is under control," Stuart said. "We've apprehended Baxter but it doesn't look like he came to kill this guy."

The police holstered their guns.

Stuart turned back to Baxter. "You were about to tell me what Desert Heat was."

"A strip club," Baxter said.

"One of the worst," one of the cops put in. "We've busted employees selling drugs there a number of times, and the strippers do a little extra work, if you know what I mean."

Alexa snorted. "It doesn't sound like you have very reliable witnesses, Mr. Baxter."

"There are security cameras. They'll show I was there. What's all this about, anyway?"

"You remember State Prosecutor Kurt Billings?" Stuart asked.

"Yeah, I know the son of a bitch."

"Well, that son of a bitch got killed last night. And so did both of the judges who put you in prison."

Baxter went pale. "I didn't do it. I swear! I may point a gun to get my way, but I'm no killer!"

Stuart studied him. His gut said the guy was telling the truth. The quickest way to find out, of course, was to check the security footage.

And he had a sinking feeling what they would find.

Another damn dead end. How many more times will the killer strike while we run in circles?

CHAPTER EIGHTEEN

Gus Hallard drove his Arizona Department of Water Resources truck down an access road alongside I-17, humming along to the country station on the radio. Despite the heat, he had the air conditioning off and the window rolled down. The hundred degree wind blasted him like a furnace, but he didn't notice.

"One hundred percent desert rat," he liked to call himself. He had lived in Arizona all his life and had worked outside all those years, first for a construction company, then for the Highway Department before training up to work for the Department of Water Resources.

He only lived outside Arizona for a few years of his life, when he had been in the Army. They'd sent him to Iraq, another desert. His friends had laughed about that.

"You ain't never going to see trees, Gus!"

Oh, he could see trees whenever he wanted. All he had to do was go up to one of the state's sky islands, the high mountains like Mount Lemmon or Mount Graham that had sweet-smelling forests and bushes and grass and everything those northern states had.

The mountains he was passing between right now were too low for that. Instead they were bare rock, a few tough cacti clinging to steep slopes, the deep canyons dotted with scrub. He'd have to drive another hour, getting onto the tableland of northern Arizona and up to Flagstaff, before he'd see any trees.

But he wasn't going that far. There was a loss of pressure at Shutoff Valve 47, just another mile up the road. Maybe a cracked seal or something. Routine repair. He saw it all the time. The harsh climate of the desert he loved so much wasn't kind to hardware.

That meant a quick and easy job and then he could get back home to Phoenix in time for dinner. Yvette was cooking up mole tacos, his favorite. The kids loved them too.

He looked down at the photo taped to the dashboard, showing his wife, a smiling Mexican-American who was still pretty in her late thirties, and his eight-year-old son Tomas and his two-year-old daughter Angelina. Both had taken after their mother and had big brown eyes and olive skin.

"You're a lucky man, Gus Hallard!" he shouted out the window.

The pull-off was up ahead. He slowed his state-owned truck and turned down the gravel road. The highway was two hundred yards to his left. Cars sped by like the meteors you saw while camping out in the desert. No one was on the access road, and the little gravel road leading to the fenced-in area for the shutoff valve never got visited except by himself or one of his coworkers.

Never? Gus slowed the truck to a stop. The shut off valve was shut in by a chain link fence topped with razor wire and a sign saying "Keep Out." But someone had used wire cutters to open a big gash in the fence. Inside, he could see water spraying out of the valve.

Gus cursed under his breath. Vandals. He'd seen it before and never understood it. Why would you break a water supply line in the desert?

He parked the truck and looked around. Whoever did this was long gone. The drop in pressure was read in the early hours of the morning, small but enough to go check. He hadn't gotten here until midafternoon, his third stop for the day. If they had enough funding, this would have been fixed already.

"Better late than never," he said to himself, hopping out of his truck and going to the bed to pull out his tool box.

He walked over to the enclosure. A big puddle surrounded the metal valve sticking out of the concrete base on the ground. A thin spray of water shot from the seal, sparkling in the sun before splashing into the puddle.

Gus examined the gaping hole in the chain link fence. Yes, done with a wire cutter. And it looked like the vandals used a chisel or something to break a hole in the valve's seal.

Kids? Probably not. They'd have graffitied the place and left beer cans around. Plus this was too far out. Kids usually vandalized sites in the more built up areas.

Militia? Yeah, probably. There were a lot of yahoos out in the desert who hated the government and tried to hurt it any way they could. Like breaking a water valve was some big victory for personal freedom! Idiots. The government sure wasn't perfect, put it kept the desert supplied with water, kept cars on highways, and did a whole bunch of other stuff besides.

Shaking his head, he splashed through the puddle, which lapped over the top of his boots, and turned the emergency shutoff. The spout of water stopped.

Now to get to work. This shouldn't take more than an hour, then it would be a big heap of mole tacos with a pretty woman and two happy kids. Gus Hallard was a happy man.

"I'd be a happier man if people wouldn't bust government property," he grumbled.

* * *

From his hiding place, he could see him. Gus Hallard was working on the valve. Hallard was right where he wanted him.

It had been a long wait. For a time he thought Hallard would never come. He'd spiked a hole in the valve in the small hours of the morning. Then he'd parked his four-by-four behind a nearby rise, taken a nap until dawn, and settled behind an outcropping of rock just twenty yards from the valve and waited.

And waited. The sun had risen high and seared him and the dry land around him. A cowboy hat and plenty of water had kept him from getting dehydrated, but it had still been uncomfortable.

That was nothing compared to the hell this Gus Hallard had put him through.

The maintenance man would have to pay for that.

Now's the time.

Hallard's back was to him. The highway was far away and no one looked out on this stretch of desert as they sped past at seventy miles an hour. The access road had only seen half a dozen vehicles in all the time he had waited. It was a risk, but he had little to lose.

He drew his knife, a long butcher's knife of the finest, keenest steel, and stood up from his hiding place.

Hallard was whistling as he worked, some Mexican tune he recognized but could not name.

While he tried to walk quietly, his boots crunched on the gritty desert floor. As he got about halfway there, another ten yards to go, Hallard suddenly stood up and turned around.

The maintenance man froze. The man who had waited in the desert for twelve hours to kill him paced forward.

Hallard put out his hands in a placating gesture.

"Look, buddy. All I want to do is fix the valve. It's for water supply. I know the government can be bad sometimes, but we need water, don't we? Why don't you boys protest at the state capitol or something?"

He doesn't recognize me. The bastard. A casual job for him, a lifetime of misery for me.

Well, we'll even that up soon enough.

He continued to pace forward, knuckles going white as he gripped the handle of the butcher knife.

Hallard stepped back, boots splashing in the puddle, then bolted forward to get out of the hole in the enclosing chain link fence.

The man who hunted him got there first, blocking his escape.

Hallard backpedaled, then fumbled in his toolbox, knocking it over with a clatter but managing to grab a claw hammer.

He raised it high over his head, his other hand outstretched as if he could ward off the knife.

"Stay back! I never did anything to you!" Gus Hallard shouted.

"How dare you say that!"

He rushed through the gap he had made in the fence the previous night, so enraged that he didn't notice one of the cut ends of the fence scrape his shoulder. He ran for Hallard, swinging his knife. The maintenance man circled around the valve, eyes wide.

"I never did anything! I got a wife and kids!"

"So did I!" the man bellowed.

The two struck at the same time. Hallard brought down the hammer as his attacker ducked to the right so that instead of hitting him on the head, he only hit him on the left shoulder, sending a jolt of pain through the murderer that cut through even his volcanic rage. At the same moment, his knife slashed deep into Hallard's side.

The maintenance man gasped, and clutched his side as the bottom half of his t-shirt turned crimson. He took a step back and raised his hammer for another blow.

But the man who had hunted him recovered first. He slashed again, cutting Hallard across the face, and again, a diagonal cut across his chest.

Hallard dropped his hammer, staggered, and tried to flee.

Mistake. The killer reversed his grip and stabbed him in the back just as he made it to the gap in the fence. Hallard grunted, fell at an angle, bounced off the fence, and back into the pool of water.

Howling with victory, the killer raised his knife overhead and brought it down on his victim's back again.

Hallard, his face in the water, coughed and raised his head, gasping out something.

"What was that?" the killer demanded, bending down, the blade dripping gore into the water. "What did you say to me?"

"Why? Why? I never did anything to you."

The killer growled and slammed the blade deep into Hallard's back. Vision clouding with rage, he nevertheless had enough self-control not to give him a killing blow.

No, he didn't stab him in the back again. He stabbed him in the arms, in the legs, then made a dozen slashes across his back. When Hallard began to lose consciousness and his face fell into the puddle, threatening to drown him, his killer pulled him to the gap in the fence so his face would be on dry ground.

Then he went back to cutting him.

Let him bleed out. Let him suffer. His suffering won't last as long as mine, but at least he will suffer.

CHAPTER NINETEEN

Alexa was going through judicial records at the police station, looking for potential suspects and getting nowhere, when her phone rang. Homicide Detective Rebstock.

"Don't tell me there's been another murder," Alexa said. Stuart, working on a computer at the next desk, looked over.

"It fits the M.O., but not the profile," Rebstock said. "A water department employee half an hour north of Phoenix got stabbed to death as he worked on some state water installation."

"Is he ex-law enforcement?"

"No. It's strange. I'm at the murder site now. I'll send you pictures. The rage that went into this killing sure matches our perp. But this is just some state water worker. It makes no sense."

"Is CSI there yet?"

"Yes."

"Is Annette on duty?" She glanced at Stuart to see his reaction, but he kept a professional demeanor. Good. He was thinking with the correct head.

"Yeah, she's here."

"Have her send us any information as soon as she gets it. In the meantime, has the family been informed?"

"We'll text you everything we get. An officer is with them now."

Alexa closed her eyes for a moment. Poor officer. There was nothing worse than taking that long walk up to the front door of a relative who thought everything was OK, that they were going to see their loved one in an hour or two and that life would just keep on going the way it had been.

She forced herself to get a grip. The sooner she and Stuart caught this guy, the fewer long walks the police would have to make.

Rebstock broke her out of her thoughts. "Send me your interview notes so I don't have to do it myself. I got enough on my plate as it is, and with this guy escalating to killing in parking lots and in broad daylight, we don't want to be doubling up work."

"Will do."

"I'm adding more men to this. Send me any of your B-list suspects for them to take care of while you go after the main ones."

"All right."

Rebstock hung up. A moment later an address appeared in her text messages.

Stuart was already up and standing by the door.

"Let's go," she said. "The killer is getting bolder, and now he's become unpredictable."

* * *

Alexa stared at Yvette Hallard as she sat on her living room sofa, clutching a family photo. She had barely looked from it when they had entered. The photo showed her with a rugged Anglo man with the deep tan of an Arizonan born and bred. A young boy and toddler were also in the smiling photo. Both of them took after their mother.

She can't look at her children and see him, was all Alexa could think.

The children, thankfully, were with friends. Alexa didn't think she could face them.

Slow tears pearled in Yvette's eyes before dropping onto the glass of the picture. The image of the happy family was steadily becoming blurred.

"Mrs. Hallard, do you know anyone who would want to harm your husband?"

Yvette shook her head. She hadn't said five words since they had arrived. A grim-faced female officer stood at the doorway, looking like she wanted to be anywhere but here.

"Was he ever in law enforcement?"

The widow shook her head again.

"Police? Security guard?" Alexa noticed a purple heart in a frame on the mantelpiece. "Military police?"

"No," Yvette whispered, her voice sounding like it came from a million miles away. "He was never in law enforcement."

Alex and Stuart traded glances. He looked as stumped as she felt.

Rebstock had sent them photos of the crime scene, and of the body. Alexa felt sure it was the same killer. No two killers with that level of rage could be on the loose in Arizona at the same time.

At least she hoped not.

"Was your husband … " she hated to ask this, but it had to be said, " … involved in any criminal activity?"

Yvette looked surprised. "No. He never ran with that crowd, even when he was a teenager. I don't think he ever took drugs in his life. He didn't even drink all that much."

Alexa looked around the living room, hoping for a clue into this man's life that might hint at why he had been next on the killer's list. Other than the purple heart, the room had mostly been decorated by Yvette. Lots of bright colors and children's drawings and photos of the dead man visiting in-laws in Mexico.

Her eyes strayed back to the purple heart. A little American flag on a stick, the kind people wave at Fourth of July parades, leaned against the frame.

For some reason, that suddenly gave her an idea.

"Has he ever served on jury duty?"

Yvette thought for a moment, then looked up. "Y-yes. Yes, he did. A few years ago."

Stuart sat up straight. Alexa leaned forward in her seat.

"What trial was this? What was the defendant's name?"

"I-I don't remember the name. This was a while ago. It was a long trial and took Gus away from his job for many weeks. He didn't mind, though. He said it was his duty as a citizen. He was even the jury foreman."

"Really?" That was interesting. The jury foreman was the one who read out the verdict. A vindictive ex-con would remember that.

Yvette looked up from the photo and stared at Alexa for a second. The desperation in her features was hard to look at.

"You think it might have been the person he put away? Oh, I can't remember the name! There was a letter, a summons. It had the case number. But that was years ago. I don't know where it is!"

She leapt up, ran over to a bureau, and started rummaging through it, tossing old bills and postcards onto the floor.

"Where is it!" she shrieked. "Where is it! Oh my God, what if I threw it away? What if we never find it?"

Alexa walked over and gently put her hands on Yvette's wrists. "It's all right. The courts keep records. We can look up Gus and find out which case he was on. We don't need the letter."

"B-but … "

"We don't need the letter. It's all right. We'll bring in that person from the trial today and question him." She heard Stuart in the background, talking on his phone. "My partner is already calling the court. We'll get the name in just a few minutes. Go sit down."

"You sure you don't need the letter?"

"It's all right," Alexa said in a soothing voice, leading her back to the sofa. "You've already done what you needed to do. You've already helped."

Stuart was already standing at the door, putting away his phone.

"They said they'll call me back in five minutes," he said.

"That was the courthouse?" Yvette said, her voice cracking.

"Yes ma'am. We'll get him."

God, I hope so, Alexa thought. *Because I can't deal with another home visit like this one.*

CHAPTER TWENTY

Alexa actually preferred to be going after a convicted killer than stay in that house of death a moment longer. She had lost a couple of good fellow officers in the line of duty, and that had been hard, but to lose your spouse, the parent of your children … that she couldn't imagine.

The court had found the record quickly enough. Eight years ago, Gus Hallard had been jury foreman on a murder trial, a trial presided over by Judge Warburton. The jury found a construction worker named Julio Matías guilty of second-degree murder, but an appeal by his lawyer on the basis of extenuating circumstances had gotten that knocked down to manslaughter. That trial was presided over by a different judge, one who was still alive. The system let him off after only seven years, the minimum sentence for that crime in Arizona. He had been released just four months ago.

Since he was on parole, they had a current address, which they sent along with the report. Efficient service. The clerk at the courthouse had heard of the killings of two judges and a state prosecutor and realized the significance of Stuart's information request.

As Stuart wove through traffic, Alexa called Rebstock.

"I'll have two squad cars join you there and you can go in together," the homicide detective said. "I'll be there too."

He then gave a rendezvous point a block from Julio Matías's house on Phoenix's rough East side barrio.

Next Alexa brought up the court records Stuart had received and had shared with her. Matías sounded like a rough customer. While he had no priors, the details of his murder trial were gruesome. A neighbor had gotten into an altercation with him and Matías had bludgeoned him with a two by four. Once he was unconscious, he had slit his throat.

Alexa shuddered, remembering that thug who had slit her partner's throat right before her eyes.

She shook that memory off.

Focus, Robert Powers always used to say. *No matter what you've seen, no matter what you're going through on the inside, you need to focus on the job. It's what will save lives, sometimes even your own.*

She continued to read.

The charge had been second degree murder because there had been no premeditation. The neighbor, angry over the fact that Matías's dog wouldn't stop barking, had jumped into his yard with a knife, intent on killing the dog. That's when Matías had picked up a board lying in the yard and knocked him out with it.

The defense claimed that Julio Matías was a quiet, peaceful man terrified that the neighbor would kill him too, and only acted in self-defense. The jury may or may not have bought that, but the throat slitting after the neighbor lay helpless on the ground was the deciding factor against him. So he went to jail for second degree murder, with Gus Hallard reading out the verdict.

Matías had a good lawyer, though, and there was an appeal. A few procedural errors on the part of the prosecution, plus the fact that the neighbor was in a gang and Matías felt he had to kill him in such a gruesome way to avoid imminent threat from the neighbor's friends, got the charge dropped to manslaughter.

Alexa shook her head. If she had been the judge she would have never accepted that ruling. But then again, she hadn't read the full court transcripts or seen all the evidence. While it looked bad on the surface, she knew she shouldn't second guess the judge's ruling. Far too often, outsiders to the system of law enforcement made snap judgements based on insufficient evidence. She had seen that with many of her fellow marshals.

So she set the judge's decision about the culpability of Julio Matías aside. What she did see of the suspect's character from what little she had time to read was that he was calculating. In the heat of the moment, with a knife-wielding neighbor leaping over the fence to go after his dog, he had picked up a two by four and bludgeoned him to unconsciousness. Fair enough.

But what came after, even if you believed Matías's every word, showed a dark and aggressive mind.

Matías had stood over his unconscious neighbor and had a choice. He could call the police and get this gang member who had trespassed onto his property with a deadly weapon arrested, and then request protection from any blowback by the guy's friends, or he could take care of it himself.

He had decided to take care of it himself, demonstrating to the gang and the entire barrio that he wasn't someone to be messed with. He must have known he would go to jail, but his honor and reputation was more important to him than his freedom. And vengeance was more important than justice.

Once he had gotten out, had he decided to prove his toughness by going after the man who prosecuted him, the juror who read out his guilt, and the judge who gave him his sentence?

Entirely possible. Normal, well-balanced people don't slit their neighbor's throats, no matter what the neighbor had done.

So how did Judge Antonio Rodriguez fit into all this? Alexa didn't know. Matías didn't have any priors. Maybe the judge in Benson had sentenced a friend or relative.

She didn't have time to check, because Stuart was already screeching to a halt at the rendezvous.

Two police cars were already parked by the side of the residential street, and Alexa recognized Rebstock's private car, a beat up old Chevy he should have replaced years ago, coming down the street.

They got out, the police emerging from their vehicles to meet them. This was a mostly Hispanic neighborhood of private houses. Some had high fences so you couldn't see in. Others had open yards but bars on the windows. No one was in sight. Alexa had the feeling everyone had disappeared when the first police car showed up.

Alexa was glad to see two of the officers were Hispanic. The court records indicated Julio Matías had used the services of a court translator. Alexa's mediocre Spanish wasn't up to the task of interviewing a probably evasive suspect, so she hoped at least one of the Hispanic officers was fluent.

Rebstock parked behind Alexa's and Stuart's vehicle and hauled his bulk out of the car. He stopped to light a cigarette and survey the area.

"OK. Let's go," he said with the casual tone of someone saying they needed to go to the supermarket. Rebstock had been on the job since Alexa had been in grade school. He had seen it all. Nothing phased him anymore.

He had obviously given orders to his officers already, because two of them went one way while one of the Hispanic cops and a female Anglo officer went with them the other way.

"Kevin and Alvaro are going through a back alley to come at the house from behind," Rebstock explained. "Just in case Matías decides to run. We'll go knock on the door like friendly little Amway salespeople."

They circled the block and came to Matías's address. It was one of those homes with a high wooden fence they couldn't see through. The gate was locked. Without a pause, Rebstock pulled out a set of lockpicks.

"Aren't we going to knock?" Stuart asked.

"Hell, no," the homicide detective said, selecting a tool and inserting it into the lock.

Stuart looked at the lockpicking operation with obvious concern. "Do you have a warrant?"

"I have a pocketful of warrants. I fill them out as I go."

Alexa smiled. Good old Rebstock.

Stuart stared at him. "Really?"

Rebstock looked at Alexa and snickered. "Feds."

"She's a fed too," Stuart said.

"U.S. Marshals aren't feds. They're cowboys," Rebstock said.

The lock clicked open. Just as it did, a furious barking broke out in the yard. Something slammed against the inside of the gate, making the whole fence rattle.

"So much for getting him by surprise," Rebstock said. He pointed to the female officer. "Open the gate a crack and see what we got."

The policewoman's eyes went wide, but she followed orders. She opened the gate just enough to see a huge Doberman, then slammed it back shut. Actually, Alexa couldn't tell if she slammed it or the giant dog pushed it closed.

"Time is of the essence, ladies and gentlemen," Rebstock said. "No time to call the animal control unit."

He pulled out from his pocket a metal collapsible rod that looked like a police baton except for the loop of rope at one end. With a flick of his wrist he extended it to a length of five feet, twisted it to click it into place, and then readied himself just outside the gate, feet planted wide apart.

"Officer Alonso, you get ready to grab this with me when I say so, but not a moment before."

The Hispanic officer got behind his boss. The barking grew louder, the Doberman's big body slamming against the gate once again.

Rebstock looked at the female officer, who had her hand on the gate. "Open it."

"You sure?"

Alexa and Stuart took a step back, drawing their guns. Alexa sure hoped Rebstock knew what he was doing, because she really, really did not want to shoot a dog.

Even that monster barking its head off on the other side of the gate.

"Go!" Rebstock shouted.

The female officer flung the gate open and leapt to one side. The Doberman barreled out. With a lightning fast movement surprising in someone as out of shape as Rebstock, the homicide detective looped the rope around the dog's neck as skillfully as any rancher Alexa had ever seen.

But the dog was huge, and the force of its charge made Rebstock stagger back. He leaned in with his weight and stopped both him and the dog, but then the animal started jerking back and forth. Rebstock almost fell over. The dog didn't seem to feel the inflexible leash at all.

Officer Alonso jumped to his aid, grabbing the pole. Gritting his teeth and planning his feet wide apart, he managed to get the animal under control. Rebstock steadied himself and helped Alonso push the dog out of the way of the gate, growling but unharmed.

"Get in there!" the homicide detective shouted.

CHAPTER TWENTY ONE

Stuart rushed through an open yard, bare of anything except a couple of half-dead shrubs. The house in the middle of the lot was a low, one-story adobe structure with barred windows. Venetian blinds blocked the view inside.

Stuart didn't even try the door, and he didn't even try knocking.

"Federal agent! Open up!" he shouted, giving the door a hard kick right next to the lock, the best place to break it.

But this was tougher than your typical American door. Not as strong as the heavily bolted metal doors you got on the average Iraqi home, but tough enough to resist his kick.

Praying Julio Matías didn't decide to shoot through the door, he gave it another kick. The door cracked but still no luck. Dimly he was aware of Alexa and the female cop flanking him, guns leveled at the doorway.

He gave a final kick, and the door flung open.

He found himself in a stuffy, hot living room. Only a single light shone, and the rest of the house looked equally dim and closed in. The sweet smell of someone smoking meth led him through to the back of the house, Stuart systematically checking each corner as if he was raiding an insurgent compound, leading with his gun, ducking low around every doorway and turn in the hall, Alexa and the female cop protecting his flanks, until he came to an enclosed back porch.

The porch was the kind that had windows all around that could be opened to let in the evening breeze, but like the rest of the house, the windows were shut, the Venetian blinds down, the air heavy with sweat and chemical stink.

Julio Matías sat on a lawn chair at one end of the otherwise bare room, a glass pipe in his hand. In a half circle around him on the concrete floor was a collection of knives, screwdrivers, hammers, and saws. In the middle of the floor sat a young woman, circled up in a ball, eyes wide with terror. A chain ran from a bolt in the floor to a collar around her neck.

For a moment Stuart stopped, stunned. He felt oddly surprised that the woman was clothed, and did not have a visible mark on her.

"Freeze!" Stuart shouted, aiming his gun at Matías.

Matías cackled, showing rotted teeth, and lit up again.

"Drop the pipe! Hands up!" Stuart ordered.

Matías took a deep inhalation. The woman babbled something incoherent.

Gut twisting, Stuart approached the man, intent on subduing him, but before he could make it halfway across the room, Alexa rushed forward, swinging down her pistol. The barrel smashed the glass pipe right out of his hands.

That seemed to wake Matías up. Shouting something in Spanish Stuart didn't understand, he leapt to his feet, only to have Alexa plant a knee in his balls.

Matías squalled and doubled over, but did not go down. The next instant he was back up, reaching for Alexa. She flipped him and he landed hard on the concrete floor. Stuart dove in and put a knee on the small of the man's back.

"I got this!" he shouted.

Alexa went for Matías, and Stuart shoved her aside. "I said I got this!"

He saw the rage in her face, and did not want her to be the star of another beating on the evening news.

Holstering his pistol, he leaned harder on Matías's back as the man shouted and squirmed.

Quickly, before Matías could recover, Stuart pulled his arms behind his back and cuffed him tight. At the edge of his vision, he could see Alexa hovering close by. He could practically feel the hatred in her, the urge to beat this man down.

So Stuart stayed close to him, not because Matías deserved his protection, but Alexa's career did.

Stuart hauled him to his feet and led him to the far end of the room. The female officer was comforting the woman, who was sobbing and speaking a mixture of Spanish and English.

"Where's the key?" Stuart said.

Matías only gave him a grin with black-spotted teeth.

Stuart shook him. "Where's the key?"

When he didn't get an answer, Stuart turned him around and patted him down. In his pockets he found a couple of baggies of meth and a set of keys.

"Here," he tossed it to Alexa.

Alexa tried a couple of keys before she found the right one. Once the collar snapped off, the woman collapsed in her arms and cried.

Stuart watched as Alexa soothed her, rubbing her back and softly saying something in Spanish. The female officer stood back, appalled at the scene.

So was Stuart. He turned to Matías.

"You speak any English?"

"Not to you, pig."

"Hold on, we'll get someone to read you your rights in a way you can understand. Even you get that."

Matías replied with what sounded like some swear words.

Just then, Rebstock came in with one of the Hispanic officers.

"Hey!" Stuart called him over. "Read Matías his rights in Spanish and tell him his under arrest for the murders and well as kidnapping."

And God knows what else.

As the Hispanic officer did so, Stuart went over the Rebstock, whose face poured with sweat.

"Where are the others?"

"Taking care of that damn dog. He's a brute."

The homicide detective sounded out of breath.

Their attention got distracted by the victim, who began to speak in English, apparently answering a question Alexa had asked.

"I came over to party, and he locked me up here. Made me eat out of the dog bowl. He said he was going to keep me as a pet until he cut me up. He sat there for days smoking and telling me how he was going to cut me into little pieces."

"You're safe now," Alexa said. "You say he's been here for days? Did he ever leave?"

"Sometimes to go to the bathroom or something, but the rest of the time he just sat here watching me. That was the worst! He never did nothing, just smoked meth and pulled on the chain and laughed at me. For days and days, just staring and laughing."

"What's the longest he ever left you?"

"Not for more than ten minutes. He'd always come back. If I tried to sleep, he'd wake me up. It never stopped!"

"How many days?" Alexa asked as Stuart got a sinking feeling in his stomach.

The woman shook her head. "I'm not sure. It's been like a nightmare. I dunno. At least three days. Four maybe."

"Are you sure?"

The woman nodded. "Yeah. Cause it was night at least three times. Nights were the worst. He'd just sit there in the pitch black talking about what he'd do to me, or creep around in the dark and kick me just to keep me from dropping off to sleep."

Stuart stifled a groan. Another false lead. They had done some good, saved a life, but the killer they hunted still eluded them.

He moved over beside Alexa.

"We need to go," he said.

Alexa nodded. "Yeah, we got work to do."

She put a hand on the victim's shoulder and said something else in Spanish, then turned for the door.

They were just getting to it as the Hispanic officer was leading out Matías.

The prisoner turned to her and smiled.

"You should have come later. I was gonna cut up that bitch."

Alexa snarled. "Why you … "

She lunged for him.

"Whoa! Whoa! Whoa!" Stuart got in between them. Alexa tried to push past, and Stuart had to grab her around the middle and pull her away. Matías only laughed.

Alexa swore at him, calling him every name in the book as the officer led him away. Matías laughed all the way out of the house.

"Easy," Stuart said. "Calm down. He's going to spend the rest of his life behind bars. He's done."

"Get your hands off me!" Alexa pushed him away. Stuart was stronger, but he let her go. He kept blocking the doorway, though.

Alexa glowered at him a moment, then turned away.

Stuart let out a breath of relief. The worst was over, but it would come back, all too soon.

He knew.

That aggression. He'd seen it so many times in Iraq. You're in a dangerous situation and you keep seeing your buddies mutilated or killed, and your mission never seems to end, never seems to get better. You can fall into a downward spiral of anger and violence.

He remembered one guy in his squad who always shouted at the Iraqi civilians. Given that they hardly ever had a translator, sometimes you had to raise your voice to get their attention, or wave them away from the convoy or gesture with your gun to get them going in the right direction. It's hard to be polite in a warzone with a language barrier. But Private Thompson took it to the next level, screaming in red-faced fury at every Iraqi who came near them. He even learned some Arabic swear words to use on them, and would spice them up with a good shove. Not a very good way to win hearts and minds. Some in his platoon shrugged it off. Others tried to talk to him about it. Stuart had reported him to his superior officer. Nothing got done.

But Stuart kept an eye on him, and when he caught Private Thompson beating a prisoner, he reported him.

This time he did get listened to. Thompson got a good talking to and was forced to see an Army shrink. He never spoke to Stuart again.

Stuart didn't think Alexa was that bad. She didn't have the casual cruelty toward the innocent or the helpless, but the anger she did have was bad enough.

She'd need to be watched.

CHAPTER TWENTY TWO

Alexa was shaking as she walked to the car. That sick bastard should be put down. Just like Drake Logan. Just like the Jersey Devil. Why couldn't they mete out justice right there and then and save the state some money? She'd watched documentaries about policing in other countries, countries so poor that most people didn't have shoes but didn't dare steal because they were terrified of the cops. That's how it needed to be here.

A small, rational part of her mind knew that she was wrong to feel this way, but damn it, she felt what she felt and she wasn't sorry.

No, that wasn't true. As they walked to the car, Alexa began to flush with shame. She had screwed up again, like with that guy Drake Logan had sent, and she didn't even have a knife wound across her chest to use as an excuse.

She looked at Stuart out the corner of her eye. He was looking down at his keys, fiddling with them to give himself something to do. They got to the car and got in.

"Back to the court records, I guess," Stuart muttered.

"Yeah, let's get to work," she mumbled, looking out the window.

They drove in silence for a time. The minutes stretched out, making Alexa feel more and more awkward. Finally she summoned the courage to speak.

"I'm sorry," she said.

"It's OK," Stuart replied, too quickly.

Alexa took a deep breath. "No, it's not. I kind of lost it back there."

"Well, if it's any consolation I wanted to beat the guy to a pulp myself."

Maybe you did, but I wanted to kill him. And not only for justice, but for my own satisfaction.

Alexa stared vacantly at the dry, desolate neighborhood of the barrio, where people were emerging from their houses now that the police had made their raid. She thought back on what Robert Powers had said in his journal, how he had felt the darkness too. Maybe lots of people were the same way.

Yeah, but they manage to keep it under control. I need to find a way to do that.

Stacy saw the video of you beating down that guy who cut you. She didn't judge you because you got attacked, but what if you blow up in a worse situation, like the one back there, and you get filmed a second time? She might not look at you with so much admiration after that.

That possibility filled Alexa with more fear than breaking into the home of an armed robber with a giant Doberman.

Stuart's phone rang. Still driving, he pulled it out, checked it. His eyes went wide and he pulled over to the side of the street, right in front of a rundown house where half a dozen guys in their undershirts were drinking beers and listening to Mexican rap.

Stuart got a boyish grin on his face as he answered.

"Hello Miss Doctor Guevara. How are you? … Oh, good. … Me? Nearly got eaten by a Doberman as big as a bus and then arrested a kidnapper. A real scumbag but not our guy. … Yes? … Oh really? That's great! Yes, please do." Alexa crossed her arms, irritated. He could at least put it on speaker, but the way his ears were turning red it looked like he wanted to keep this between the two of them. "Yes … OK … about that dinner. When I solve the case? What if Alexa solves the case, are you going to have dinner with her?"

Stuart burst out laughing. Alexa could hear Annette laughing on the other end of the line. Then she said something Alexa couldn't hear.

"Ooooh …" Stuart gave Alexa a sly grin as she frowned back. "I see. Well, I think that's a good idea. Yeah, got to go. Thanks a million. Bye."

"So?" Alexa said as he hung up.

He laughed, irritating Alexa even further. "She says you're too serious for her, and you're a boring straight girl anyway. But she says not to worry, because she's looking for a guy to hook you up with. She says that would help you lighten up," Stuart laughed again.

"What did she say about the case?" Alexa asked, her annoyance rising.

"Oh, the case! Right," Stuart looked disappointed, like he wanted to keep talking about Annette. "She says the knife wounds and some footprints they found make her sure it's the same guy. He was wearing Timberlands this time, same size as the sneakers he had on when he killed Billings. Also, he scratched himself when he went through that gap in the fence. She found a couple of threads of a light tan cotton shirt and, even better, some traces of skin."

Alexa sat bolt upright, her irritation vanished. "DNA!"

"Yes. She's extracting a sample right now. Might take some time to run it through the database, and of course if our perp was from an older case they won't have him in the database, but it's still a win."

Alexa nodded. It was rare that you found enough direct evidence to convict someone outright, especially with a person this clever. But with a DNA sample, they could corroborate a suspect's presence at the scene. That would be enough to convict.

They still had to find a suspect, though.

A clinking on the glass of her window made her look around. One of the guys from the porch had come up to the car and was knocking on the window with his beer bottle. His friends stood in the yard, halfway between the house and the car. They all looked pissed off.

Alexa realized that with the sun in his eyes and the slight tint to the window, he couldn't see she was wearing a uniform.

"You're in our spot," he said loud enough to be heard through the closed window. "Move your ass!"

"I'll handle this," Stuart said, unbuckling his seatbelt.

"No, I will," Alexa said.

"But—"

Too late. Alexa was already opening the door.

She stepped out and stood in front of the guy, ending up almost touching him. She had to look up to look in his eye. Quite a long way up.

"Can I help you?" she asked in as polite a tone as she could muster.

His gaze flickered across her uniform, resting on her chest for a moment.

Seriously? You're staring at a cop's breasts?

He seemed to remember himself and looked her in the eye. "Uh, sorry officer. It's just that we're expecting a friend and we need this spot."

"All right. We're just stopping for a minute. But I don't want you getting all aggressive with strangers in cars, you hear me?"

"Yes, sir. I mean ma'am. Officer."

Alexa pointed to his beer bottle. "And you're in violation of Phoenix's open container law."

The guy quickly retreated to the lawn.

“That’s better,” Alexa said, getting back in the car. “Have a nice day.”

“Uh. You too.”

Stuart chuckled as they drove off. Alexa hoped that display of professional self-control had lightened the mood somewhat, but she knew her partner wasn’t going to forget the ugly scene back at Julio Matías’s house.

And then there was the main problem—they still didn’t have a suspect. While Rebstock’s people were checking some of the less-serious suspects, Alexa didn’t hold out much hope for them to get lucky.

Alexa stared out at the passing houses, wracking her mind for an idea.

Always look for the outlier, Powers used to say. *Look for what doesn’t fit. Because when you can explain that, you’ve found the answer to your case.*

“We need to look closer at Gus Hallard,” she said. “He’s the outlier here.”

Stuart nodded. “He’s never been in trouble with the law. I checked. You can’t take the wife’s word for it, but she was right. Served in Iraq too.”

This last statement came out quiet. Thoughtful.

Alexa got on her phone, texting the clerk at the courthouse who had gotten them the information about Hallard’s jury duty so quickly.

“Check for any records regarding Gus Hallard, no matter how minor,” was all she said.

The answer came back almost instantly. “Dropping what I’m on and will do this now.”

Alexa leaned back, feeling a warm sense of belonging. This was one of the best parts of being in law enforcement. People pulled together, everyone from homicide detectives to court clerks. Stuart probably felt the same about his platoon when he served in Iraq.

“Maybe we’ll get a hit,” Stuart said. “Oh, I checked that old murder trial in Benson, the one where Judge Rodriguez let that drifter off. Turns out that guy died a year ago in Los Angeles.”

“That’s one less loose end.”

“Yeah, but not much of one. No reason he’d carry a grudge. I felt it was worth looking into. I also told the Phoenix P.D. to dig into why a loser like Derek Baxter was able to cough up half a million in bail money. Turns out he got his parents to put up their house as collateral."

"That's some bad parenting right there," Alexa said.

"Big time. They've probably been spoiling that idiot from day one. I hope they don't end up losing their house if he skips bail. Speaking of parenting, how's that kid of yours?"

"Stacy? She's not my kid."

"Could have fooled me."

Alexa laughed. "I should call her. I haven't talked to her in more than a day."

"You should. Nothing like talking to family for some R and R. My parents have passed, but I call one of my brothers every night before I go to bed. Or my cousin. She's almost like a sister."

"That's nice."

Alexa thought of her own family. Her brother Malcolm was a nervous wreck and struggling to recover from several addictions. Her other brother Wayne was busy with the ranch all the time, and his reporter wife had called Alexa so many times in the past day that she had blocked her number. And Alexa's dad was … her dad. She loved him, of course, but they never saw eye to eye on anything. Since Robert Powers got killed, though, he had been trying to reach out. She had to give him that.

Stuart was right, though. She should make more time for all of them. Especially Stacy. Things were easy with Stacy despite the teenybopper drama and her drunk parents.

Alexa's phone buzzed with an incoming email from the court clerk.

"That was quick," Alexa said.

Quietly working in the records office and just as dedicated as I am.

The email contained an attachment, a record of a murder case from ten years before, when Gus Hallard probably hadn't been married yet. He had been on jury duty again, although not as foreman. Alexa saw right off why the clerk had missed it on the first run through the records.

The case had never gotten past jury selection. The defense had found that the prosecution had tampered with evidence and the judge declared a mistrial.

The prosecuting attorney was Billings. He managed to avoid being disbarred for evidence tampering because they couldn't prove it was him and not one of the arresting officers.

The judge presiding was Judge Warburton.

The suspect, an independent long-haul truck driver named Mark Storrs, had several priors for affray, drunk and disorderly, possession of marijuana, and threat with a deadly weapon. He had been tried in courtrooms all throughout southern Arizona.

Including in Benson, by Judge Rodriguez.

Then another detail popped out at her. The case had been dismissed without prejudice, meaning it could be brought back into court without it coming under the definition of double jeopardy. Legally, the case had been suspended, not dismissed. There was generally a statute of limitations for a situation like that. In the case of the State of Arizona vs. Mark Storrs, that statute of limitations ran out in a week.

Had Storrs been killing off the judges and prosecuting attorney in the hopes of not having to face that murder charge again?

That didn't make sense to a logical mind, but they were dealing with a maniac. Who knows what twisted logic the guy was working under?

And then there were all his other crimes …

Alexa scrolled through the long list of judges, prosecuting attorneys, and jurors, a chill running through her. The killer's work might be far from done.

CHAPTER TWENTY THREE

Alexa peered through a pair of binoculars at the distant trailer, her elbows resting on the hood of a Highway Patrol vehicle. She had, of course, called for backup.

The trailer stood alone off the side of a little-used county road an hour west of Phoenix. Sitting on dry flatland, it had an unobstructed view of a vast area of almost featureless rock and grit plain, a few low mountains in the hazy distance.

Mark Storrs obviously wanted solitude. The nearest convenience store was ten miles away, the nearest town twenty. No other houses or trailers were in sight.

Beside the little undersized trailer there was a battered old pickup truck, a large blue plastic water tank, and a portable solar panel. Storrs looked like he was planning to stay a while.

Alexa did not like the looks of this place. There was no way to approach without the suspect spotting them. In fact, he might already be looking at them through his own binoculars.

At least there was only one road in and out. Of course, Storrs might decide to take that pickup truck over land. While it looked pretty old and was not a four-by-four, the tires were new and the terrain pretty flat.

Alexa hoped they wouldn't end up in a car chase across open desert.

"I don't really see any other way of approaching this situation except driving on up there and using the highway patrol's loudspeaker to tell Storrs to come out with his hands up," she said.

Hopefully he won't come out shooting instead.

"Yeah," one of the highway patrolmen said, looking grim. He obviously didn't like the tactical situation either.

But everyone present was paid to do things they didn't like, so they piled in the cars and drove at a moderate pace toward the little trailer, eyes alert for any sign of someone hiding in the low gullies or behind the rocks scattered around the area.

Nothing moved until they stopped in front of the trailer, one highway patrol car parking sideways across the little lane connecting his lot to the county road, the other a bit down the county road in one direction, with Alexa and Stuart parking a bit down the other way. The idea was that if Storrs cut across his front yard to get to the county road, these cars would be able to head them off.

The curtain in the trailer's lone window lifted a little.

The highway patrol's loudspeaker rang out across the silent desert.

"Mark Storrs. This is the police. Come out with your hands up."

Alexa's own hand rested on her pistol. Stuart had his hand inside his jacket, touching the grip of the gun in his shoulder holster.

The curtain in the trailer fell back into place. A breeze blew across the barren land, making a hollow, lonely sound.

"Mr. Storrs. Come out with your hands up, along with anyone else who is in the trailer or hiding on your property."

The door to the trailer opened. Alexa's grip on her gun tightened.

Mark Storrs was a short, squat man with curly black hair that needed to be cut a month ago. He wore faded jeans and a white t-shirt. The arms he raised above his head were thick and powerful. Some sort of pendant hung from his neck and flashed in the sun.

The suspect walked slowly toward the patrol car blocking his driveway. When he got about ten yards from the car, and well away from his own vehicle and trailer, the police ordered him to halt.

"Let's do this," Alexa said.

They climbed out of their car and walked across the bare desert toward him, the crunching of their shoes on the grit the only sound. The two highway patrolmen stood in the drive, their guns trained on Storrs. The other two highway patrolmen remained in their vehicle, ready to pursue if he tried to run.

Alexa decided not to draw her gun. They already had him covered and when getting in close with a suspect, it was generally better to have both hands free. Stuart, by unspoken agreement, also kept his gun inside his jacket.

As they drew closer, Alexa could see a gold cross hanging around Storrs's neck.

"What's all this about?" he asked as they came up to him.

"We just have a few questions. Put your hands behind your back."

"Am I under arrest?" Storrs asked, doing as he was told.

“You are being held for questioning,” Alexa replied, snapping on the cuffs.

Stuart patted him down and found nothing. Two of the highway patrolmen sauntered up.

“Put him in the back of your car,” Alexa told one of them. “Once we search his place we’ll take him to your station and question him.”

Stuart nodded to the other patrolman and they headed over to search the truck and trailer.

Alexa followed the first patrolman and Storrs to the police car.

“So what are you doing all the way out here?” she asked.

“Living the quiet life,” he said. “I have trouble dealing with people. The psychologists say it’s social anxiety disorder. Never have gotten along with people very well.”

“I know. I’ve seen your list of priors, volumes one, two, and three.”

Storrs shook his head. “I’m all through with that now. I stay out here where it’s quiet, and only come into town to go to church or pick up my rig to go on a run. I’m scheduled to drive to San Diego tomorrow. Am I going to make it?”

I doubt it.

“We’ll see,” Alexa said.

“Church has helped,” Storrs said. “So has working alone.”

They got to the highway patrol vehicle and stopped.

“Can you attest to your whereabouts for the past week?” Alexa asked.

“No. I’ve had the week off. I don’t get much work in the trucking company. I’m a fill-in. I don’t need much money, though, so it suits me fine. Why? What’s going on?”

“Do you remember Judges Warburton and Rodriguez, and State Prosecutor Billings?”

Storrs nodded, his features hardening, eyes getting evasive.

Now we’re getting somewhere.

“Do you remember a juror named Gus Hallard?”

“No. Was he at one of my trials?”

“The one that got thrown out in mistrial.”

“The cops set me up,” Storrs growled. “They had it against me.”

The highway patrolman chuckled. “Oh yes, you’re an innocent victim and have never done anything wrong.”

Storrs gave him a sharp look. “I’ve done lots of things wrong. Messed up my life from the get go. But I’ve never killed anyone. The cops saw my priors and made up their minds. So they fudged the evidence to make a conviction."

"Billings didn't have a part in that?" Alexa said, trying to lead him.

Storrs shrugged, the chains on his handcuffs rattling a little.

"Maybe. Probably not. The cops are the ones who do that kind of stuff. Those slick city lawyers don't like to get their hands dirty. So what's going on with those people you mentioned?"

"All four of them are dead," Alexa said, studying his face as she said this.

Mark Storrs's eyes widened in surprise. "All of them? How?"

The reaction seemed genuine, but she'd met a lot of criminals good at faking.

"Stabbed," she snapped, looking into his eyes. "One by one. You wouldn't happen to know anything about that, would you?"

"God rest their souls," Storrs muttered. More loudly he said, "I am not a killer, and I forgave the people who put me inside when I took Jesus into my heart. They were only doing their job and I was guilty as sin."

"Guilty of murder?" the patrolman asked.

"No, not guilty of that," Storrs answered hastily. "And I haven't forgiven the policemen who tampered with evidence to try and put me away for a crime I did not commit. I have enough sins to atone for without adding killing to my soul's burden."

"You trying to tell me you haven't heard about all these murders?" Alexa asked. "They've been all over the news."

"I don't listen to the news. It depresses me. Makes me anxious," Storrs said.

Alexa stared at him, unsure what to think.

After a moment of silence, she motioned to the officer.

"Put him in the back of the car. I'm going to help with the search."

First she came up to the officer rummaging through the pickup truck.

"Not much to find here," he said. "Registration is up to date. Plates check out. No drugs or weapons. I'm going to search the rest of the property. No room for two of us in that little trailer."

"All right," Alexa said, moving on to the trailer.

The officer was right. When she got to the open doorway, she saw Stuart took up almost all the spare room. There was only a narrow space between the bed, with some cupboards on top, and a tiny shower and kitchenette on the other side. On the wall above the bed was a poster of a UFO.

"He might be right about not hearing the news," Stuart said. "No TV. Probably can't get reception all the way out here. A little radio tuned to the evangelical station. No newspapers or magazines. Damn, what does he do all day?"

"Good question. Find anything else?"

Stuart grinned, holding up an evidence bag containing a butcher knife.

"The same dimensions as the one our murderer used," Stuart said. His smile faltered a little. "Of course I have one the same size myself. So do lots of people. Maybe the lab folks will find something on it."

"Hope so. Anything else?"

Stuart made a helpless motion around the little trailer. "No drugs. No maps or paperwork to tie him to the crimes. No bloody items of clothing. Oh, I checked his size with that old set of sneakers over there. Size ten. Not ten and a half, but he could have worn larger shoes to put us off the trail."

"Maybe," Alexa said.

"Maybe," Stuart muttered. "I'm almost done here."

"The patrolman is searching the area. Didn't find anything in the truck."

Stuart put his hands on his hips and looked at Alexa. She felt like she could read his thoughts.

He was worried this was another dead end, just like her worry.

They'd know better once they had checked him out down at the station and reviewed that old case.

CHAPTER TWENTY FOUR

Back at the station, Alexa delved into the murder Mark Storrs was tried for while Stuart oversaw the suspect's processing. They were also doing a DNA swab that would be sent off to the lab for crosschecking with the skin fragments Annette Guevara's team had discovered.

What she read in the case file made her doubt that Annette would find a match. If Alexa had had time to study these case records before arresting Storrs, she wouldn't have been so convinced they were about to catch the killer.

The trial was from almost exactly ten years before. The body of a thirteen-year-old girl, Heather Dawson, had been found one monsoon season half buried in sand and driftwood.

The same age as Stacy. Damn.

Her body had been thrashed around by the torrents that come with the summer rains and had become bloated with decomposition. It took dental records to identify her.

Heather Dawson had been stabbed to death. Although the knife was a smaller one than the one used on the current murders, the enraged slashing and stabbing were the same.

There were no signs of sexual assault, but with a body that far gone it was always difficult to tell. The CSI team didn't recover any physical evidence from her killer or killers. No doubt she had been thrown into a wash in monsoon season for the specific purpose of cleaning the body and moving it away from the scene of the murder.

Cold and calculating, just like the killer they hunted.

Next she went through the evidence against Mark Storrs. They had found a pair of girl's panties in his apartment, the kind teenagers would wear. He claimed it came from a petite prostitute who played younger roles. The police and prosecution claimed they were identical to the ones worn by the victim. Storrs, of course, could not produce the prostitute to collaborate his claim of where he had obtained them. That made things look good for the prosecution.

The problem was that the panties had been washed. No DNA. Also, they were a simple white cotton with pink trim. Too common to make a close comparison. The father of the victim said they had written her name on the labels of all her clothing when she went to camp earlier that summer. The label on the panties in Storrs's apartment had been snipped off.

Once again, things looked good for the prosecution, until the defense noticed that in one of the police photographs of Storrs's apartment where the panties were sitting in a drawer, the tip of the label could be seen poking out from the waistline.

The label had been cut off *after* the police had collected it as evidence.

Once the defense revealed this to Judge Warburton, Storrs was a free man.

Because without those panties, the prosecution had little else. Storrs had a bad reputation as a criminal and occasionally a violent one, but he had no history with the victim, no history of sexual violence or kidnapping, and only a couple of witnesses could vaguely put him roughly in the right place and time to have kidnapped Heather.

Alexa checked the later documents for any new evidence that had cropped up. There had been none. It seemed the murder of Heather Dawson would remain unsolved.

Alexa bit her lip. She hated that word. "Unsolved." What that meant for the grieving family was "unresolved." What it meant was a lifetime of misery and uncertainty.

Stuart came in.

"The DNA swab is done. I've also ordered swabs for all the other fine upstanding citizens we've interviewed."

"Kind of grasping at straws, isn't it?"

Stuart grunted. "Yeah, but straws are all we have to grasp at. I'm thinking he's not our man. I don't have anything solid to back that up; it's just that I get the feeling he's actually turned a new leaf."

"I think you're right. Look at this report. Even before someone messed with the evidence, the prosecution was facing an uphill battle. And no new evidence has come to light. Storrs has no real reason to fear the case would be reopened. No one has suggested that it should. It's been in the cold case files for a while now. Storrs hasn't been in trouble with the law since the trial."

"He said something about that to me. He said that nearly being charged with murder made him wake up to the kind of life he was living. That if he continued the way he was going he'd end up dead or in jail for life. So he turned to God. And you know what? I think I believe him. I've heard plenty of cons claim they've found Jesus and keep on committing crime, but this guy's turned squeaky clean."

Alexa turned to the case file. "Then how does this trial fit? I have a feeling we're getting close … " She snapped her fingers. "Wait. What if we've been looking at it the wrong way?"

"What do you mean?"

"Remember how you said we should be looking at present and future cases and not just old ones? What if that's not it? What if we shouldn't be looking at the criminals at all?"

Stuart blinked. "Then who would be looked at? The—"

They said it at the same time.

"The victims!"

Stuart got a distant look. "Someone who didn't see justice done and has decided to make it himself."

He threw himself into a chair in front of the spare computer and began bringing up old newspaper articles about the murder. Alexa started going through police files, checking the names of everyone in the jury, and everyone in Dawson's family, for records.

She didn't have long to look.

Tim Dawson, the victim's father, had been picked up for disorderly conduct six months after the trial had been dismissed.

"Stuart, look at this. Heather's father was found on a Phoenix street screaming and kicking in windows. When police detained him, he shouted that he had seen Mark Storrs walking down the street. He couldn't stand seeing that the man was living a normal life and blamed police for letting his little girl's killer go free. There's also a note here that he had recently gone off his antidepressants."

"So Tim Dawson falls into depression after losing his daughter," Stuart said, brow furrowing. "He's got a grudge against the judge for letting Mark Storrs go free. He's got a grudge against Billings too, for messing with the evidence and ruining the case."

"There's no proof Billings did it," Alexa said.

"Proof doesn't matter at this point. The guy is blaming everyone."

"Sure," Alexa said, nodding eagerly. "His depression gets worse. He's put on meds, and we both know how often those don't work as planned. I can't count the number of times I've had to deal with people whose meds didn't work right or who had gone off them and had a bad reaction. Then he sees Storrs walking the streets a free man and he snaps."

"But why not kill Storrs? Why go after all these other people?"

Alexa thought a moment. Yeah, that didn't make sense.

Wait, yes it did. Storrs was living in the middle of nowhere, cut off from almost everyone. He would have been a hard man to track down. And if Dawson couldn't find him, what was the next best thing?

"He wants to pin the killings on Storrs. Make him go to jail for murder, like Dawson thinks he should have in the first place."

"Oh. Wow. Hey! That explains why he went after Judge Rodriguez. Storrs, in this role, would want to take revenge on all the people who put him in jail. Also, Dawson would want to punish Storrs's previous judges who didn't keep him in jail."

"Wow, we're really dealing with a sick mind. And why go after Gus Hallard? He was on the jury for Heather's murder but never got to make a ruling. The case was dismissed."

"We know the killer has been researching his victims," Stuart said. "He's been planning this for a long time. Tim Dawson must have researched the jurors too, and found that Hallard gave someone a guilty verdict in a murder trial. That must have stung, considering that in this other murder trial the suspect went free."

Alexa leaned back in her chair and said in a hushed, fearful tone, "Then his circle of potential victims could be limitless. He could go after the arresting officers, the other jurors, all of Storrs's previous judges. It could go on and on!"

Stuart turned to the computer and started tapping away. "We need to find him. Now."

"Wait. First we need to find the next victim. Warn him. Dawson might be there already."

Stuart looked at her, confused. Then the light came on in his eyes. "The defense attorney. The one who found the label had been removed. He'd be the highest on Storrs's list now! Higher than Hallard even. There must be some reason he went after the juror before the defense attorney."

"He waits for a good opportunity. Maybe he couldn't get the defense attorney in an easy spot but discovered that Hallard worked alone in the desert."

“Right.” Stuart got back to the computer. “Here it is. Court records show the defense attorney, Andrew Teagan, living here in Phoenix. Oh, he hasn’t appeared in court for the last two weeks until today.”

“Maybe he was out of town on vacation. That would explain why Dawson wasn’t able to target him.”

Stuart grabbed his phone. “And he just got back. Dawson would know that. And it’s already getting dark. He’s going to want to strike tonight.”

Stuart punched in the number for the defense attorney’s office.

“Hello? May I speak to Andrew Teagan? He’s gone? This is Stuart Barrett of the FBI. Is he really gone? Yes? I need his personal phone number. I have reason to believe he might be in danger.” Stuart frowned. “What do you mean how do you know I’m really FBI? Haven’t you heard about those judges and that state prosecutor getting killed? Give me that damn number!” Pause. Stuart started scribbling down a number. “All right. If he calls, tell him to call me back at this number immediately.”

Without pausing to speak to Alexa, Stuart dialed Andrew Teagan’s personal number. Alexa could hear it ringing. And ringing. The beep of a voice mail came on.

“Andrew Teagan, this is Special Agent Stuart Barrett of the FBI. We have reason to believe that Tim Dawson, the father of Heather Dawson, or some other person related to one of your cases might be targeting you for a revenge attack. We suspect the same individual might be behind the series of attacks on court officials in recent days. Please, if you get this message, call me back immediately, and get yourself and your family into your car and drive to the nearest police station.”

Stuart hung up and turned to Alexa.

“Shall we call Dawson? Go to his house? He still lives in Phoenix.”

“Did Teagan’s office have any idea where Teagan might be?”

“They said he usually goes straight home after work. He left just five minutes ago.”

“Let’s pull up his office and his home address on Google Maps.”

They checked, and found with the tail end of rush hour traffic it would take him half an hour to get there, assuming he didn’t stop at the supermarket or somewhere else.

Next they checked Tim Dawson’s last known address. It was closer than Andrew Teagan’s house.

“Let’s go,” Alexa said.

Within seconds they were in the car and pulling out of the police station parking lot, Stuart gripping the wheel and Alexa calling for backup.

CHAPTER TWENTY FIVE

The Dawson home stood in a quiet little cul-de-sac. The house itself was modest, with a well-tended lawn that, despite the tense situation, still managed to irritate Alexa. Why in the world did people insist on having grass lawns in the desert? Didn't they know the state had chronic water supply problems?

That made her think of Gus Hallard, the water department worker whose only crime was serving as a juror like any good citizen. This quiet, nondescript home might very well hide a crazed killer.

At least they would have him outnumbered. Rebstock's battered old Chevy appeared at the end of the street, coming their way. He had radioed them during their crazy drive across town to say he had picked up a patrolman and was coming in his own vehicle. Two unmarked cars were unlikely to spook Dawson if he looked out the window.

Alexa's uniform was a problem, though. For the first time in this hot, stressful few days, Alexa felt jealous of Stuart's suit.

She got on the radio. "Rebstock, how about you have the officer circle around back to make sure Dawson doesn't run that way?"

"Already dropped him off there. And you keep behind Agent Barrett and me. Maybe he won't spot your uniform."

Alexa chuckled. "Took the words right out of my mouth. It's like you read my mind."

"I actually can read minds. That's how I've put so many people away."

Alexa grinned, then gave a worried glance at the house. She still felt nervous about this. Dawson, if he really was the killer, had always used a knife, and he did not have a licensed firearm, but that didn't mean they couldn't end up on the wrong end of a gun.

Rebstock parked in front of them and got out, moving his considerable bulk to stand between the house and the car door. Stuart got out first, and Alexa tucked herself behind the two men.

"No movement from the house that I can see," Rebstock said, lighting a cigarette. He took a drag and let out a long, hacking cough.

"Those things will kill you," Alexa said.

"Not if some criminal kills me first."

"On that cheerful note, let's go check on Tim Dawson," Alexa said, putting her hand on her gun. The two men had shoulder holsters, their guns hidden by their jackets.

The three of them walked across the street. A female jogger huffed down the sidewalk, stared at them, and increased her pace.

They came up to the front door. Rebstock flung his cigarette to the side, squared his shoulders, and rang the bell. It sounded out like the chimes of Big Ben. Alexa would have laughed if this wasn't so serious.

Movement behind the door. The porch light switched on. The peephole in the door darkened as someone looked through it.

Stuart is going to have to kick another door in. How many does that make now?

"Who is it?" a female voice said.

Rebstock pulled out his ID and held it up. "Phoenix police department."

There was a click as the door unlocked. Then it opened.

They saw a woman in her fifties with deep sorrow lines on her face and bags under her eyes. Immediately Alexa knew they were facing Heather's mother. She had seen that look before, that of the endlessly bereaved.

"Hello, I'm John Rebstock, homicide division. This is Deputy Marshal Alexa Chase and Special Agent Stuart Barrett of the FBI. What's your name, ma'am?"

"Goodness! What's going on?"

"Your name, ma'am."

"Ursula Dawson."

"Is your husband Tim at home?" Rebstock asked.

Ursula Dawson looked at each law officer. "What's this about? Have you found new evidence about Heather?"

"I'm afraid not, ma'am. We'd like to talk to the two of you about the case, though." Alexa kept a poker face. Rebstock wasn't exactly lying, after all.

"I'm afraid he's out. He's on his evening jog."

"Where?" Alexa asked.

"Oh, around the neighborhood. He takes different routes. He probably won't be back for half an hour. Can I take your number?"

"May we come inside, ma'am?" Rebstock asked.

"I don't see why not. So what's happening with the case? Are you reopening it?"

Rebstock didn't reply as all three of them walked in. Since she had allowed them inside, they didn't need a warrant.

By unspoken agreement, Stuart and Rebstock moved further into the house while Alexa, being the only woman, stayed with Ursula.

"What are they doing?" Ursula said, looking nervous.

"They just need to search the house, ma'am."

"Has Storrs made threats? Is he coming to get us?"

"No. Actually I'd like to tell you that Mr. Storrs is currently in custody. We're investigating some crimes that he might be involved in. You have nothing to worry about."

Ursula let out a gust of relief. "That man is an animal. I remember in the trial when the prosecution read through that long list of crimes. I knew it was only a matter of time before he got arrested again."

"At the moment he's just being held for questioning, ma'am," Alexa said, keeping an ear cocked for any shouts or sounds of a struggle.

She also kept an eye on Ursula. The woman looked nervous, but not overly so.

If Tim is the killer, he hasn't told her. That would be smart, of course.

"So why do you want to speak with Tim?" Ursula asked.

How the hell do I answer that?

"We're, um, concerned he might have had contact with Mr. Storrs."

"With that killer? We never want to see him for the rest of our lives. You know what happened to Tim after he was let free?"

A little. Not enough.

"What?"

"He had a nervous breakdown. Well, we both did. But his was worse. He slipped into a deep depression. We saw a psychologist, but what could the man say? We had lost someone so close. It felt like *we* had been killed."

Alexa found herself tearing up. "I know how you feel."

A flicker of annoyance passed over Ursula's features. "I hate it when people say that. How could you possibly—"

"Did you hear about that U.S. Marshal Drake Logan killed the month before last?"

"Yes," Ursula replied, concern softening her face.

"That was my … " Alexa's voice choked, " … my partner."

Ursula put her hands on Alexa's shoulders, and Alexa almost lost it.

Alexa pulled back as quickly as she could. She was on a case. Stuart and Rebstock might be in danger. She had to keep it together.

She straightened up, cleared her throat, and nodded thanks to Ursula.

"It's hard," Ursula said. "And it takes a long time to get easier. After a point, it doesn't get easier at all. You just learn to live with it. Come. Look at this."

She led Alexa into the living room. They could hear Stuart and Rebstock moving around upstairs, still searching the house.

On the mantelpiece was a large picture of Ursula, a man her age and a girl of about eleven. They sat in a boat with a giant fan on the back, surrounded by a swamp.

"We went on vacation to the Everglades a couple of years before we lost her. She loved the airboat ride. She was laughing and cheering the whole time. The driver even let her steer for a while. We went to an alligator farm too where she got to feed them. I remember how scared she was, but she insisted on doing it. She was such a brave girl. Always up for an adventure."

Several other photos showed the progress of an older girl from age about fifteen to twenty.

"Who is this?" Alexa asked. "Your other daughter?"

Ursula gave a faint smile. "In a way, yes. It's our niece. My brother's daughter. She lived in Phoenix until she went to NAU for forestry. Now we go up to Flagstaff to spend time with her."

"So you sort of adopted her?" Alexa asked, thinking of Stacy.

"Not quite. We had to restrain ourselves. After the first few really bad months, we spent more time with all our family. That sort of tragedy brings a family together. And we started spending more time with Samantha. Of course my brother and his wife could see what we were doing, and they were very kind to let us. Tim and I agreed to hold back a bit. We would have loved to have spent every moment with her, but our psychologist warned us that wouldn't be healthy. She was right. Funny, I never believed in psychologists until I needed one."

"I see," Alexa said. She had two unanswered calls from Joan on her phone.

Ursula went on. "So we went to her basketball games and took her out for ice cream. That sort of thing. We limited ourselves to two days a week. Tried not to spoil her on Christmases and birthdays. Samantha understood. She's been very good about it. When we go visit her in Flagstaff she takes us hiking."

"I'm glad you found someone," Alexa said.

"It doesn't replace Heather. Nothing can. But it helps. If you lose family, you just have to find more."

Alexa nodded. *Family is what you make it.* Stuart had said that, referring to a younger kid he met in school who had become like a little brother to him.

Rebstock and Stuart came back downstairs.

"He isn't here."

"I told you, he's out jogging," Ursula said.

"We have to check, Ursula," Alexa said. Stuart looked at her when she called her by her first name.

"Did he bring his phone with him?" Stuart asked.

"No. It's right over there on the coffee table."

Rebstock took it.

"We need to check Andrew Teagan's place," the homicide detective said. "Let's head over there now. Ma'am, I'd like you to stay here and call this number immediately if you see or hear from your husband."

Ursula took the card he gave her. "Why? I don't understand."

"Just routine, ma'am."

Routine, hell, Alexa thought. *You're hoping you're wrong as much as I do, but you think you're right.*

Sadly, so do I.

As they headed out the door, Alexa tried calling Teagan again.

Still no answer.

"Stuart," she said, worry cutting her voice as Ursula watched from the doorway, "I think you should drive a little bit quicker this time."

CHAPTER TWENTY SIX

Now for the next punishment.

Tim Dawson sat in his car opposite Andrew Teagan's house. In this neighborhood there were no parking restrictions like in some developments, and as long as you parked on the street and not someone's driveway, no one cared.

To the outside observer, Dawson's car was unoccupied. The engine and lights were off, and the tinted windows kept anyone from seeing that he sat inside.

But he could see. He could see everything.

Andrew Teagan's Mercedes was just pulling into his driveway. Dawson gripped the knife hidden under his shirt, aching to rush out and cut him down right then and there.

Teagan got out, a fit, thin man in his late fifties who spun his key chain around his finger as he always did when he was in a good mood.

Bastard. Living a happy life when he got a murderer off Scot free and left the victim's family in perpetual misery. He'd soon fix that.

In an unconscious movement, Dawson's free hand went to the door. At the last instant he stopped himself from opening it. That would have turned on the interior light, and Teagan might spot him.

He had to wait. Because parked next to the Mercedes was an SUV. Teagan's wife drove that. He didn't want any witnesses, and he didn't want to kill anyone innocent.

He wasn't like Teagan, or the others. He was on the side of right.

It wasn't like he had long to wait, he told himself. Teagan's wife was about to leave.

Tim Dawson had done his homework, as usual.

Casing the house a few weeks ago, he had spotted a sticker for an evening soccer camp on the SUV. Looking up the camp, he found it was for grade school and middle school kids. The website even listed the hours when the sessions took place. Since he knew Andrew Teagan often worked late, it stood to reason that his wife generally took the kids to camp.

The park was a twenty-minute drive away. The classes only lasted an hour. So it stood to reason that Mrs. Teagan would either stay at the park watching the practice or go do some shopping and return to get them. She would not come back home only to have to turn around almost immediately.

Dawson knew enough about Andrew Teagan's schedule to know that he often came back around the time the camp ended or a bit before. This meant that the defense attorney would often be alone at home for a time in the evenings. It was amazing how much you could find out about someone just with a bit of research.

But what about tonight? The lawyer had gotten off early. Would he drive the kids to soccer? Tim would lose his chance at vengeance.

He'd find out soon enough. Tim Dawson glanced at his watch. Any minute now.

There.

The front door opened. Dawson gritted his teeth to see Teagan appear in the illuminated rectangle of lamplight, then he let out a sigh of relief. Teagan had his shoes off.

The wife appeared. They kissed and she walked out. Teagan turned to face the interior of the house and called out, "Boys! Come on, you're going to be late."

Perfect. Only a matter of a few minutes now, and Dawson could scratch one more evil man off his list.

Two boys appeared, about twelve and ten, dressed in the camp's uniform of dark blue shorts and matching top. The older boy had a ball tucked under his arm. The lawyer waved to his kids and shut the door.

Teagan's wife pressed on her keychain and the SUV beeped and unlocked, the lights flashing once.

The older boy kicked the ball up into the air and stopped its fall with his forehead. It bounced up again, he shifted a little backwards, and bounced it off his forehead again.

Tim Dawson watched, a sudden lump coming to his throat. Heather had played soccer too. She loved bouncing the ball like that.

Tim had gone to every game. To be honest, he had been a bit bored of it all at the time, but now every one of those games was a treasured memory.

The younger boy rushed up to him and shouldered him aside. The ball fell to the ground and he laughed.

“You spaz!” the older boy shouted without anger and tried to get the ball back.

The smaller boy was too quick for him, and darted to the other side of the lawn, his older brother in hot pursuit. For a moment they tussled, then the older boy let out a triumphant whoop and made off with the ball.

“Boys, come on!” Mrs. Teagan said.

The younger boy made to chase him, then abruptly switched directions and ran for the SUV.

“Shotgun!” he shouted.

“No way, spaz. It’s my turn.”

“Too late!” The nine-year-old had already hopped in next to his mother.

“It’s my turn!” the older boy whined, suddenly sounding nine himself.

“Never mind. You can sit in front on the way back,” Mrs. Teagan said.

The older boy picked up the ball. “Ugh! He’s such a dork!”

“I’m better at Call of Duty than you!” the kid teased from inside the SUV.

“Only because you’re a sweaty try hard.”

“Jealous!”

“Mom, we going to the water park this weekend?” the older boy asked as he opened the back door and threw the ball in.

“We’ll see.”

“Yeah! The water park!” the younger brother said, suddenly in league with his rival.

“We have a lot to do this weekend,” their mother objected.

“You can leave us there.”

“Yeah, totally! You can leave us there.”

Whatever the result of the debate, Tim Dawson missed the rest of it. The doors to the SUV shut, and Mrs. Teagan backed out of the driveway. Within less than a minute, the vehicle had driven out of sight, and Tim Dawson was alone with his next victim.

But the killer wasn’t looking at the SUV or the house, he had his forehead against the steering wheel, sobbing.

Seeing kids always got to him. Tim couldn’t work anymore, because he couldn’t stand to see the family photos on the desks of his coworkers. He couldn’t go to the supermarket, couldn’t go to the park.

He barely left the house. When he did, he'd look away if a child passed, especially a teenaged girl. Even with his eyes averted he'd tense up, feel the old pain return.

Watching those two boys play in their front yard had overwhelmed him. It had only been for a minute, perhaps less, but it was like a knife in his heart, twisting and gouging.

He sat in his car, forehead on the steering wheel, trying to pull himself together.

Maybe he shouldn't go through with it. Teagan had two kids. How would it affect them when they came home and saw their father lying in a pool of blood?

They would feel like he felt, when he had to go to the morgue to identify Heather's body and found there was nothing left of his beautiful daughter to recognize in the bloated, waterlogged, half-eaten corpse.

Tim's head shot up and he glared at the house, every muscle coiled to spring, like a rattlesnake when its lair is invaded. Teagan had gotten Storrs off. He had knowingly defended a child murderer. He had dug and dug until he found a tiny little irregularity in the prosecutor's case that he could blow way out of proportion in order to get the case thrown out of court.

Sure, Billings had falsified evidence, but he had done it to get Storrs convicted. His crime was to do it so badly that Storrs went free instead.

Teagan's crime was to point out this error and help get Heather's killer out.

In in the years since, how many killers had he gotten free? Look at this nice house in this nice neighborhood. Way better than anything he and Ursula had, especially after he couldn't work anymore. They had sold their old home—a place haunted by memories of a happy life—and had been forced to downscale. Meanwhile people like Billings and Teagan got rich off injustice.

Teagan deserved to die. They all deserved to die.

But those two boys …

What kind of men will they grow up to be with someone like Teagan as a father? They'd be better off without him. Sure, it will hurt in the short term. That was a pity and Tim felt sorry about that. There was no avoiding it, though. Teagan had to die.

"Maybe I'll take him away from the house," Tim said to himself. "That way the kids don't have to see him."

Feeling better about himself, Tim Dawson took a quick look around to make sure the coast was clear and got out of the car. In his hand was an Amazon package he had stolen from the front porch of some house in Tempe. He wore a brown shirt and slacks and matching baseball cap. There was no logo, but Tim had long ago learned that a familiar prop and the most basic of disguises was all you needed to fool the casual observer.

The only off note was the gloves. Who wore those in Phoenix in summer? But he had to avoid leaving fingerprints.

He checked his knife was in position and walked across the darkened street straight up to Teagan's front door.

Tim rang the doorbell. After a moment he heard Teagan's voice. "Who is it?"

"Amazon delivery."

"That was quick!"

Teagan smiled. So he really had ordered something from Amazon. Perfect.

Tim bowed his head slightly as if checking the label. That way the brim of his hat would hide his features.

The door opened.

For a moment Tim stood frozen. Here he was, the man most responsible for letting Storrs go free. The man who had doubled his misery. How could he ever find peace when Storrs went unpunished?

"Hi! Thanks for this." Teagan held out his hand. When Tim still didn't move, confusion began to mask the attorney's face.

Tim tossed the package past him into the front hall.

"What the—" Teagan turned to watch it skid along the tile.

Tim pushed him from behind, making Teagan stumble. That gave Tim enough room and time to step inside, close the door behind him, and draw the knife from under his shirt.

Teagan turned and froze, mouth wide open.

Recognition came to his face.

"Oh my God. It's been you," Teagan gasped. "You killed the judges. You killed Billings!"

"And I'm going to kill you," Tim growled.

Teagan didn't resist. All he did was shake as Tim came up, slammed him against the wall, and put the knife against his throat.

"P-please. I got a wife and kids."

"I've heard that before."

"Don't hurt them. Do whatever you want to me, but let them go."

That reminded Tim of the promise he had made to himself. Those boys couldn't come back to see their father as a bloody mess in the front hall.

"All right. I'm taking you out of here. If you struggle, I'll come back for your family. If you shout, I'll come back for your family. Got it?"

"Y-yes."

"Pick up that Amazon package." It had the address of the house where he stole it. That was a clue as to Tim's movements. Not much for the police to follow up, but Tim hadn't gotten this far by being careless.

Teagan looked confused.

"Pick it up!" Tim shouted.

Teagan raised his hands and moved over to the package. Tim followed right behind. The lawyer gave a nervous glance over his shoulder and picked it up. Tim snatched it from his hand and held it over his knife.

"There, now your neighbors won't see. Now open the door and walk across the street to the car parked there. I'll be right behind you. Any funny stuff, and your family will come back from soccer practice to a very bloody front lawn. I might just decide to stick around too. Now move."

"Where are you taking me?" the defense attorney asked as he opened the front door.

Good question. Tim thought for a moment as they walked outside. He glanced around. No one in sight except for a car half a block away driving in the other direction.

Then the idea hit him.

"You're going to drive," Tim said.

"Where?"

Tim Dawson smiled. "The perfect place."

CHAPTER TWENTY SEVEN

Alexa clenched the dashboard as Stuart sped through traffic, Rebstock and the police officer just behind in the other car.

Looking out the front window was a bit like watching a video game as Stuart wove through traffic.

"Can't you put on a siren or something?" Alexa asked. "You're in an unmarked car, you know. Someone might try to drive us off the road."

"We don't want to warn the suspect," Stuart said.

"What if someone road rages and tries to shoot us?"

"We'll just have to take that chance," Stuart said, knuckles white on the wheel. He cut off a semi, making Alexa squawk.

The police radio crackled.

"Rebstock to Chase and Barrett."

Stuart reached for it, but Alexa slapped his hand away and grabbed it from him.

"Concentrate on the road," she said.

"OK." Stuart made another swerve and Alexa jerked to the left. Their heads clonked together.

"Cut it out! I'm driving here."

"Jesus Christ," Alexa muttered. Gripping the handset in one hand and the back of the seat in a vicelike grip, she replied to the homicide detective, "Chase to Rebstock. What is it?"

"I had dispatch call for support units. No show. There's been a shooting nearby and all available units had to respond. We'll have to handle it ourselves."

"Life in the big city. Give me the countryside any day."

She thought about Ursula and stopped the joking around. In the best case scenario, this poor woman was about to face the lawyer who got Storrs off. In the worst case scenario, she was about to discover her husband was a murderer.

Alexa sat back and buckled her seatbelt. Once all this was finished, should she try and talk with Ursula? Tell her that as an officer of the law she thought Storrs was innocent, and that he even seemed to have turned over a new leaf?

No. She doubted Ursula would listen. The Dawsons were convinced Storrs was guilty; it had become part of their psyche. Changing that would be extremely difficult.

Briefly Alexa wondered how she would be dealing with Robert Powers's death ten years from now. Of course it wasn't the same as losing a child, but she had seen him killed right in front of her eyes in the most gruesome fashion. Would that searing vision ever fade?

With a final swerve between two cars coming the opposite direction, Stuart pulled into a residential street and slowed.

"Second street on the right," the cop in Rebstock's car said over the radio. He had been paying attention to Google Maps while Stuart and Rebstock drove like maniacs. If those two had taken their eyes off the road for an instant, they'd all be dead and probably a few other people too.

Stuart picked up the handset now that he was going at a sane speed. "You still back there?"

"Just coming around the corner now. You know how many moving violations I could cite you for?"

"Only a few more than your boss committed. You'll have to cite both of us."

They pulled up at Teagan's address. There was no time for stealth now, no time to get into position, they simply stopped in front of the lawyer's house and got out.

One car was parked in the wide driveway, although a small oil stain told them the Teagans had a second vehicle.

"I called Teagan's office and cell phone," the patrolman said as they moved toward the front door. "The office said he left nearly an hour ago and he's still not picking up his cell phone."

They rang the doorbell. No answer. Rebstock glanced at them, wrapped his hand in a handkerchief, and tried the door.

It was unlocked.

"Stay out front in case Dawson hasn't gotten here yet," the homicide detective told Alexa. He drew his gun and he and Stuart rushed inside. The police officer moved to the backyard.

Alexa stepped out onto the front lawn and looked up at the windows. No movement. Then suddenly she saw a man pass into view.

Her heart leapt and her hand went to her gun, but a moment later she saw it was Rebstock.

She glanced around the neighborhood. No sign of anyone except a curious neighbor peeking through the blinds.

"No one's here," Stuart said, coming back to the front hall. "No signs of violence. The wife and two kids are gone."

The police officer came around from the back of the house. "I just checked the plates for the Mercedes here in the driveway. It's Teagan's. His wife has an SUV registered in her name."

Alexa turned to the officer. "Look up Tim Dawson's vehicle and put out an APB."

The policeman got to work.

"There was no sign of a struggle," Rebstock said, coming out of the house.

"But where is he? And where is Dawson? I think he's already been here and gone."

Stuart frowned. "Maybe. But if he has been here, why not kill Teagan in his house? Why abduct him?"

Everyone thought for a moment.

Stuart looked around. "This house isn't as isolated as the other murder locations. Maybe he wanted to take him somewhere where they wouldn't be heard."

"Somewhere symbolic maybe," the patrolman said.

"Or maybe he was worried the wife and kids would come home," Rebstock suggested.

Suddenly, Alexa snapped her fingers. "That's right, you said there were kids living here."

"Two boys, from the looks of it," Rebstock said.

"Think of it. Tim Dawson lost a kid. He wouldn't want to kill his victim anywhere where kids are present. He killed Hallard out in the desert. The other victims either had grown children or no children. Dawson doesn't want to hurt the kids."

Stuart snorted. "Then maybe he shouldn't be trying to kill their father." He took out his phone and pulled up Google Maps. "Where could he have taken him?"

The three of them stared at the phone.

Stuart had put Teagan's house dead center of the map. Seen from a bird's eye view, Alexa traced the winding streets of this upper class housing development, and nearby a wider, straight thoroughfare lined by strip malls.

"Maybe behind one of those malls?" Rebstock suggested. "Plenty of dark space there with loading docks and dumpsters and such."

"I'm thinking this park here," Stuart said, pointing at an expansive green space. "It looks pretty big. He could find a quiet spot to take Teagan."

Alexa's knowledge of Phoenix brought up another possibility.

"Pull out a bit," Alexa said.

Stuart did, and on the northern edge of the image appeared the straight line of a concrete-lined channel used to funnel rainwater during Arizona's monsoon season.

"There," she said, pointing. "His daughter Heather was found in a wash, and this is the closest thing to a wash you'll find in central Phoenix. In fact, it probably was a wash before they paved and straightened it."

"Could be," Rebstock said, nodding. "A bit of a stretch, though."

"It's all we've got to go on," Alexa replied.

"We'll go to the mall," Rebstock said, gesturing at the patrolman. "And we'll try to get some cars to go to the park."

"Let's go," Alexa said.

She was already running to the car. If she was right about Tim taking the defense attorney, they didn't have a moment to lose.

In fact, they might already be too late.

CHAPTER TWENTY EIGHT

Tim Dawson smiled with righteous satisfaction. He had gotten away with it again. No one had seen him abduct Andrew Teagan, and nobody stopped them as he had made Teagan drive the car to the wash, the point of Tim's knife at his side.

They parked behind a crafts shop that had closed for the night. Behind it ran the concrete-lined wash. As he forced Teagan to get out, he gazed at the darkened storefront and teared up.

"Heather used to love crafts," Tim whispered. "When she was smaller she always had glitter everywhere. Her hands, her face, all over her school notebooks, everywhere except where she wanted to put it. I used to call her My Little Glitter Girl. We used to laugh so much."

"Mark Storrs didn't kill her," Teagan said.

"Quiet," Tim snarled, poking him in the back with the knife to keep him moving forward. Oh, how he'd like to ram it into this smug, slick lawyer's back. Right up to the hilt!

He struggled to keep control, hands shaking with rage and anticipation. He had to get Teagan out of sight. He had to stay free so he could finish his work.

Nothing was more important than that. Nothing.

They moved along the bare concrete side wall of the store toward the open side of the wash just behind. Tim kept the point of his knife, carefully hidden underneath the Amazon package, in the small of Teagan's back. He glanced over his shoulder. A few cars passed by but nobody stopped. As long as he kept his weapon out of sight, no one would notice anything. People went about their own affairs, unknowing and uncaring of what happened around them.

They got to the edge of the wash. It ran straight through the neighborhood, about twenty yards wide and ten deep, with sloping sides they could easily get down.

It was dim here, only the lights of the streets to either side filtering distantly over the bare stretch of concrete. Here and there glittered shards of glass from broken beer bottles. Candy wrappers and plastic bags rustled in the wind. Not far off, a shopping cart lay on its side. On the opposite side of the wash, Tim could see the back of a strip mall. Two blocks to the left, a bridge spanned the wash. Three blocks to the right was another one. Too far for passing motorists to see in the relative gloom.

"Go down there," Tim said.

"Please. I have a wife and two children."

"I had a child once."

"Then you know! You can't—"

"That's enough out of you," Tim growled. At least he tried to growl. His voice broke as he the words came out.

When Teagan didn't move, Tim jabbed the knife into his back. Not hard. Just enough to break the skin. The lawyer yelped and scrambled down the slope. Tim followed.

Teagan picked up speed, pelting down the concrete slope.

"Help!" he shouted.

"Oh no you don't," Tim said.

He rushed after him. For a moment it looked like Teagan, spurred on by terror, would get away, but then he cried out, stumbling. He tried to continue running but began to limp.

Tim smiled. The lawyer was still in his socks. He must have stepped on a piece of the broken glass.

It took only another couple of seconds to catch up to him. A quick slash across his back brought him down. Teagan fell hard on the concrete, turning over and raising his arms and legs like a dog begging for a belly rub.

"Don't do it! Don't do it! Show some mercy!"

A red haze settled over Tim's vision. The chase and the sight of Teagan's bloody sock from where he had stepped on the glass, brought out the bloodlust in him.

"Mercy? Did Mark Storrs show any mercy to my daughter? Did you show any mercy to me and my wife when you got him off? Why you—"

He went in for the kill. Teagan kept his arms and legs up to shield his body. One by one Tim slashed at them, cutting them so hard the treacherous defense attorney couldn't keep them up to defend himself. Then Tim ducked down, grabbed him by the hair, and raised him to a kneeling position.

* * *

Stuart had no idea where on this damn dry river they should go. It stretched for miles right through the city.

Next to him in the car, Alexa was on the police radio.

"I don't think he'll go far," she said. "We're going to go to the closest point and search there."

"Sounds good," Rebstock said. "But remember he wouldn't go too near any of the bridges. How about this? You stop between the bridges along 4th and 9th Streets. Once we check the park, we'll cut back past 4th and check out the wash there."

"Right. Over and out."

"This is a longshot," Stuart said, blowing through a yellow light.

"Yes it is," Alexa said.

"And if he's not in the park, they won't get back here in time."

"No they won't," Alexa confirmed.

They heard Rebstock's voice over the radio calling for backup.

"I hope that shooting is over and done with and we can get some more units to respond," Alexa said.

"Yeah, so where should we stop?"

They were just passing a liquor store that was still open. The bright lights and two cars out front made that seem like an unlikely choice. Up ahead was a long strip mall, most of the shops closed. Beyond that they saw a sign for a crafts store.

"Stop in this strip mall," Alexa said. "He could easily hide his car behind here."

Stuart swerved into the parking lot and squealed to a stop, ending up across three parking spots. Alexa had jumped out even before he had switched off the engine.

She paused for a moment, caught in the headlights of the car, then bolted for the corner of the building.

When Stuart opened the door, he immediately knew why. He could hear a man screaming faintly in the distance. It sounded like it was coming from beyond the strip mall.

Alexa ran around the corner, heading for the dark swath of the wash between the strip mall and the road on the other side. Stuart followed.

He sprinted around the concrete building past dumpsters and heaps of trash and came to the edge of the long concrete-lined channel. Alexa stood at the edge, looking around. Another shout made them both jerk their gaze to the right.

About four hundred yards down the wash, behind the craft store, two figures stood in the half-lit bottom of the wash.

Or rather, one knelt and the other stood behind him.

Was that a knife Stuart saw? He wasn't sure, but he sprinted along the edge of the wash along with Alexa.

"Federal agents! Tim Dawson, stop right where you are!" Stuart shouted.

The two figures froze.

There's no way we're going to get there before Tim stabs that guy, Stuart thought, *and I can't risk a shot from this range. I'm just as likely to hit Teagan.*

Surprisingly, they did not hear the defense attorney cry out. He was slumped, obviously injured and being held up by the murderer. It looked like all the fight had been cut out of him.

They made it about half the distance before they heard someone shout, "Don't come any closer!"

They kept running, testing him.

The standing figure raised the knife high, its long blade catching the distant streetlight.

"One more step and I'll slit his throat."

Stuart and Alexa stopped in their tracks.

"You can't escape!" Stuart said.

Actually he could. I didn't even have time to radio our location. And if he sees me pull out my phone, Teagan is a goner.

"Stay where you are," the figure said.

"Tim Dawson?" Alexa asked.

Before the man with the knife could speak, Alexa's question was answered by someone else.

"Tim! What are you doing!"

Stuart spun around. Ursula. She had followed them.

Stuart's heart sank. They had left the suspect's wife alone with her vehicle. What a stupid thing to do. The fact that they didn't have the time to do anything else didn't help the situation. Now a tense standoff had become ten times as complicated.

"Ursula? What are you doing here?" Tim cried.

"I followed them here. What's going on? You said you were out jogging. Have you really—"

"I'm sorry I lied. I did it to protect you. I've been getting Heather justice," Tim's voice sounded irregular, pleading. The sight of his wife at one of his murder scenes had obviously upset an already unbalanced mind.

"Justice? This is crazy!" Ursula shrieked.

Stuart lowered his gun in order to look less threatening. He couldn't make a shot from this distance anyway. Alexa's gun remained holstered.

"It's not crazy, Ursula. I was crazy before, when I sat back and did nothing while Mark Storrs walked around a free man. You know how bad I was. Couldn't work. Couldn't concentrate. And all those damn antidepressants numbing my mind."

Tim's voice choked off. Was he crying?

"You mean you haven't been taking them?" Ursula started walking along the side of the wash. When Tim, who still had the knife to Teagan's throat, didn't object, Stuart and Alexa cautiously followed.

"No. My mind is clear now." Considering the position he was in, he said this with a terrifying serenity. Explaining himself to Ursula seemed to have a calming effect. Not that it would stop him from killing Teagan, and Stuart doubted they could stop Tim or take him alive.

"You know what the doctor said if you went off—"

"The hell with the doctor! He's just part of the whole damn system. If he wants me to have peace of mind, he should have helped find Heather justice. But I've done it myself, Ursula. I've done it all."

"You mean … "

"Yes. I got back at the judges and the prosecutor and even one of the jurors. I guess Teagan will be the last. But I got all the main ones. They can fry me if they want. I don't care. I got Heather justice."

"No one is going to fry anybody, Mr. Dawson," Stuart called out. They were still about eighty yards from him, far too distant to risk a shot. "Why don't you let Mr. Teagan go and we'll talk it out."

"Talk what out?" Tim demanded, his voice rising to the edge of a scream. "These people let the murderer of my child go free. I saw him once on the street, just walking along and whistling. *Whistling*, like he didn't have a care in the world. While me and Ursula had to live in misery."

"Then why not kill him?" Ursula said. "Why kill all these other people?"

"Don't you see? It's to get him the jail sentence he always deserved."

"What do you mean?"

"He had a mistrial without prejudice. It can be restarted, but that term runs out at the end of the week. By killing these people, I could get Storrs tried for their murder."

And it almost worked, Stuart thought. *This guy, as crazy as he is, played us.*

They still slowly approached. Stuart was surprised Tim didn't object, but he seemed so obsessed with justifying his position to his wife that he didn't care. Or maybe he knew he was caught and it didn't matter.

"But Tim, you're killing innocent people! And you lied to me! Saying your car was in the shop, saying you were going for long walks at night. How could you hide all this from me? We should have talked it through."

"I did it to protect you. Now that I'm caught, the police will only take me. You're blameless."

He's going to stab Teagan before he goes down. Maybe if I can get just a little closer ...

Fifty yards now. Still too far to take a shot with a pistol in bad light at a target half obscured by a hostage.

Still they approached. Stuart cocked his ears for the sound of more police arriving, but all he heard was this desperate couple talking about their world falling apart for the second time in their lives.

"Tim, these are innocent people. How could you!"

"These are not innocent people. Billings cut the tag off Heather's panties to make it look like Storrs had done it. All that did was make it look like he *didn't* do it. Billings was a drug addict, Ursula. I've been watching him for months. His mind was so addled with coke he screwed up the case."

"But the judges ... "

"Judge Warburton let Storrs go, and Judge Rodriguez had the opportunity to put Storrs away for earlier crimes but gave him a light sentence, giving him a chance to prey on innocent people again. And this piece of trash—" he gave Teagan a shake as the lawyer moaned "—he was the one who helped get Storrs off. He's the guiltiest of them all. No, Ursula, they are not innocent."

I notice you didn't mention Gus Hallard, you nutcase, Stuart thought. *Kind of hard to justify killing a father of two who did nothing but sit on a jury that never made it to a ruling.*

Stuart allowed himself to trail a bit behind, getting Alexa in between him and the perp. Could it be that Tim hadn't noticed his gun, being too busy justifying himself to his wife and keeping an eye on Teagan? They continued to draw nearer, and sooner or later Tim would wake up to the danger. Stuart wanted to delay that as long as possible.

They only made it another few steps before Tim called out, "That's far enough!"

Everyone stopped.

"What are you going to do, Tim?" Ursula asked in a low voice.

"What I set out to do."

Teagan sobbed.

"Don't do it, Mr. Dawson," Alexa called out. Stuart kept himself half hidden a few feet behind her. "If you let him go now, we'll go easy on you."

Stuart would have bet a thousand dollars no one believed that. This guy was going to get the death penalty if he didn't cop an insanity plea, and everyone there knew it.

And it sure didn't sound believable. Alexa's voice came out in a low growl, the tone halfway between a command and a threat. She was losing patience, like he had seen his partner do on a number of occasions. And when she lost patience she would step over the line.

They couldn't afford that right now. One sudden move, one threatening gesture, and the lawyer was a dead man.

But Alexa must have been hoping Tim would believe it.

He did not.

"Do your worst!" Tim shrieked. "I'm dead anyway. I've been dead for ten years!"

He pulled back his arm, Ursula screamed, and Tim plunged the knife into Teagan's back.

The lawyer let out a grunt and fell flat on his face.

And then several things happened at once.

Tim raised the knife triumphantly, turning it around in his hand so that he could plunge it into the man lying at his feet.

Stuart stepped to the right to get a clear shot at him.

Alexa started to draw her gun …

… and Ursula grabbed it.

The marshal was taken by surprise as Ursula leaned her weight into Alexa's arm, turning her away.

Turning her toward Stuart.

The gun barked. Stuart felt a hot streak of pain and doubled over.

CHAPTER TWENTY NINE

Alexa let out a cry of shock as she saw Stuart fall, shot by her own hand.

"Let my husband go!" Ursula shouted.

Alexa took her finger off the trigger, jerked her gun hand up to get the weaker woman off balance, and used her spare hand to land an uppercut to her jaw.

Ursula staggered back several feet and fell hard on the pavement.

Alexa took a quick glance at Stuart and saw him sinking to his knees, a dark stain spreading across the side of his dress shirt. Panic rose up in her.

No. I can't lose another partner. I can't let someone else down.

Then that panic turned to rage.

She turned back to Tim Dawson.

For a moment he had paused, probably as stunned as anyone by what had just happened, then raised his knife again to give Teagan another stab.

With a snarl, Alexa aimed and fired.

And missed.

She had fired high to avoid the chance of hitting the lawyer, but ended up missing Tim as well.

The killer turned and bolted, angling to the right in order to get behind the slope of the wash to hide his retreat.

Alexa managed to turn back to Stuart and found him still standing, crouched and clutching his side with one hand, his gun with the other.

"I'm OK," he gasped. "Go get him!"

Alexa hesitated, anger and worry fighting for supremacy. "But—"

"GO!"

Alexa scrambled down the sloping side of the wash and saw Tim a good fifty yards ahead, running for all he was worth.

She sprinted up to where Teagan lay. As she approached, he shifted a bit and moaned.

Stay with him or go after Tim Dawson?

She kept running. She didn't have her first aid kit on her and she knew Stuart would be calling this in already. Rebstock and/or another unit responding might have even heard the shots. There was nothing she could do for Teagan that wouldn't be done by someone else within a minute or two.

Besides, she had a killer to catch. No one had a chance of catching Tim Dawson except her.

She focused on running. Tim was ahead of her, but kept looking back over his shoulder, losing his rhythm. Alexa slowly began to gain on him.

Tim began to zigzag. At first Alexa didn't understand why, but then realized he was afraid of getting shot.

But officers of the law, despite what some people thought, didn't shoot indiscriminately. She could not gun down a fleeing suspect.

Even though she really, really wanted to.

Tim didn't realize this, though. His mind was so poisoned by vengeance, he must have thought everyone acted on their urges like he did.

Like I almost have. Like Robert Powers almost did.

Yes, there's a darkness inside all of us. The real difference is between those who can control it and those who give in to it.

Alexa felt like shouting out to him to give up, that his wife was lying injured back there. But she needed to conserve her breath. He wouldn't listen anyway.

She picked up the pace, slowly gaining on him.

Suddenly Tim angled to the left, heading for the other side of wash. A large drainage pipe, almost the height of a man, fed into the wash on that side. Above, on the street level, was a gap between two buildings. Alexa could see the lights of a busy street with several shops open.

If he goes into the pipe, he might be able to jump me from a side channel. If he goes up to the street, he might grab an innocent bystander.

I can't let that happen. I have to shoot him.

But I can't shoot him, not just because of the regulations but because of me.

He's the one who kills people from behind, not me.

God, it would feel good though.

She quickly scanned the area, hoping to see some police officers heading him off. There was no one. It was only her.

Alexa turned her gun to aim down the length of the wash and fired. That was the least likely direction for a stray to hit someone.

Tim ducked and looked over his shoulder. By the time he did, Alexa had the gun facing him. He never knew she had not fired at him.

"Do you want Ursula to end up alone?" Alexa shouted.

She wanted to sound menacing, rather than worried. Enraged, rather than hopeful.

And she did.

Because she was sick of this whole sad scene. Sick of selfish people who struck out at everyone else to cover up their failings and ease their unhappiness. Yes, Tim Dawson had been a victim, but he stopped being a victim the first time he had picked up a knife.

Now he was just as guilty as whoever had killed his daughter.

All the pity this man deserved had been replaced with contempt. While Drake Logan had been a killer, he had been driven by a grand and maniacal vision of humanity. As sick as he was, he really thought he was improving the world. Tim Dawson, on the other hand, was just a sad, selfish man lashing out at the world in order to make himself feel better. In his desperate bid to escape justice, he had even abandoned his wife.

Alexa felt like putting him down, like you did to a horse with a broken leg.

Dawson hesitated. Alexa paced toward him until she was just a few steps away. He stared at the gun, then back at the drainage pipe, still a good ten feet away.

"Drop the knife," Alexa ordered.

Tim's face twitched. His upper lip curled, baring teeth. With a roar he charged her.

Alexa aimed right between the eyes. His insane, twisted face seemed to loom up at her, encompassing her entire vision. She could not miss.

Suicide by cop? Not today.

Alexa brought her aim down just as he reached her and shot him in the leg.

Tim cried out, stumbling and falling. His head hit Alexa in the stomach. She staggered back, her gun going off a second time, the bullet panging off the concrete.

Tim ended up flat on his face. The knife skittered away.

Alexa rubbed her stomach, wincing.

Tim pushed up with his hands, trying to rise with a useless leg. He looked around for his knife.

Ignoring the pain, Alexa rushed over to him, put a knee on his back, holstered her gun, and cuffed him.

Just as she finished, the sound of running feet made her look up and put a hand on the butt of her gun.

Rebstock was huffing across the wash for her, his jowly face sweating, smoker's lungs heaving, a revolver in his hand.

"I got him," Alexa said. "Go check on Stuart. He's been shot."

"He deserved it," Tim groaned.

Alexa looked down on him. "What did you say?"

"Anyone who tries to stop the course of justice deserve to die."

"On second thought," Alexa said, standing up and forcing herself to put some distance between her and the prisoner, "Why don't you take care of him, Rebstock. I got more important people to worry about."

* * *

The ambulance flashed its spinning lights as it pulled away with Tim Dawson in the back, sedated and under guard. Behind it went a police car. In the back, slumped and handcuffed, sat his wife Ursula, arrested on charges of assaulting a police officer.

Alexa watched them go with mingled emotions. Ursula had panicked and done a foolish thing. Stuart had been hurt, and for that, Alexa could never forgive her. But the better part of her nature hoped the judge wouldn't go too hard on her. She had suffered enough. Prison, yes, but not for too long.

For Tim, she felt no pity. He had forfeited that when he had turned from victim to perpetrator.

Instead she turned her attention to the second ambulance that had responded to the call. Stuart lay in back, an IV drip in his arm as he joked with the EMTs, working through the nervous aftershock of being under fire. She had seen that in herself and her fellow officers far too many times. The bullet from Alexa's gun had ploughed a furrow in his side and he had lost some blood, but had not turned out to be serious. He would be fine.

But that did not make going up to him any easier. It had been her gun that had fired the shot, after all.

Just as she could never forgive Ursula, she could never forgive herself.

Just a couple of months after losing one partner, she had almost lost another.

Here she was trying to protect the innocent from evil, and she ended up endangering the people who fought on the side of good.

She had almost lost it back there, not paying enough attention while she went full-bore at the bad guys. She needed to get her head on straight. She needed to be more careful.

Alexa squared her shoulders, cleared her throat, and walked up to the back of the ambulance.

"Stuart, I'm so sorry," she blurted before she had even got there.

His face turned grim. Slowly he shook his head.

"I don't know how I'm going to live with it," he said.

A lump rose in her throat and her stomach fell through the pavement. "Look, she got the jump on me. She—"

"The pain," he groaned. "I just don't know how I'm going to deal with the pain."

"I know. I'm sorry." Alexa climbed into the ambulance.

"My head is going to kill me."

"Your head? What—"

"From the hangover I'm going to have from all the beers you're going to buy me!"

Stuart and the EMTs burst out laughing.

Alexa smiled, but then felt tears welling up in her eyes.

"Whoa, whoa," Stuart said. "Hey, come here."

Wiping her eyes, Alexa shifted closer to Stuart. The EMTs suddenly found things to do that required them to look in the other direction.

As Alexa sat down next to Stuart's stretcher, the FBI agent took her hand, a strangely intimate gesture from a guy who preferred to joke around.

"Look. You got a scare. We all get scares on this job. And it's coming so soon after the worst shock of your career. I get it. But I'm fine, and it wasn't your fault. I was taken in by Ursula Dawson too. Hell, she really was innocent, at least until she saw what her husband was doing and decided to help him out. Good thing he didn't confide in her from the start, or our investigation would have been ten times as hard."

"But—"

"No buts. We got the bad guy, and Teagan is going to live. They told me that stab in the back missed all his vital organs. And the other wounds were superficial."

Alexa nodded. The EMTs had told her the same thing. "Yes, but I should have been watching her more closely."

"You were too busy watching the knife-wielding maniac. So was I. If you want to blame yourself for Ursula getting the jump on you, then you have to blame me too. And I'm not taking blame for that. The only thing I'll take from you is a few gallons of beer."

Stuart squeezed her hand.

Alexa chuckled and squeezed it back. "How about I do one better? I'm sure you're getting some time off for this. How about a weekend at my family ranch? Dad always has a fridge full of beer and my brother Wayne is an ace at a BBQ grill."

Stuart moaned and lay back on the bed. Alexa bent over him, panic rising in her.

"Are you OK?"

"OK? Hell, no! I got to spend a weekend getting sunburned and being bitten by rattlesnakes? I'm going back East where it's civilized!"

CHAPTER THIRTY

The Chase ranch in northern Arizona, one week later ...

Alexa sat on the front porch, a tall glass of lemonade at her side and Robert Powers's journal on her lap.

She had been dipping into it on and off for several days. Its pages contained a treasure trove of insights and wisdom, and a lot about her former partner she had never suspected.

Despite reading it for several days straight, she was only a few pages in. She didn't burn through it like she did sometimes with novels to get her mind off work. Instead she read only a page or one day's entry at a time, savoring it like fine wine. She learned more that way.

Even in death, he was still her mentor.

And she had plenty of time in which to think about what it contained. Because of the shooting, she had been given two weeks' paid leave while it was investigated. This was no threat to her job, just standard procedure. She and Stuart had sat in front of a review board giving their accounts of events, and the review board had looked on with sympathy, especially after Stuart had strongly defended her actions. There would be no blowback for accidentally shooting her partner.

That comforted her. The journal comforted her even more.

One entry read, "Finally caught that escaped convict. I felt bad, because we had a choice of two leads to follow and I picked the wrong one. Once we caught him, I realized the lead I should have followed was obvious. A case of 20/20 hindsight. In fact, at the time both leads looked equally plausible. I need to stop beating myself over the head about stuff I can't control. Nobody is perfect, especially not at this job. You just have to accept your failings, try harder next time, and keep on going. Just remember that doing this job makes a difference. That's the important thing. Being imperfect just comes with the job.

"Like *that's* going to make me feel better!"

The last bit made Alexa chuckle. It warmed her heart too, knowing that her personal hero struggled with the same issues she did.

And you're a personal hero to Stacy. Maybe you should stop trying to act perfect with her and let her realize you're sometimes as scared and confused as she is.

The girl's laughter rang out in the distance. She and Alexa's brother Malcolm had gone for a ride.

She sure isn't scared and confused right now, Alexa thought. *Get that girl around horses and she's the happiest kid in the world.*

This was the third time Alexa had brought the kid up for the weekend. She loved the horses, the fresh air, and the distance from her parents, who never objected to their neighbor taking their kid out of the house for a couple of days. It made it easier for them to party.

Stacy even liked the work. Alexa's father bossed her around like she was an unpaid ranch hand, and she didn't mind at all. He'd become an adopted grandfather, gruff but loving. Stacy had never mentioned her own grandparents. Stacy didn't mention a lot of things about her family life.

A spark of sunlight off metal made her look out over the desert. A car was making its way slowly along the dirt road leading to the ranch, trailing a plume of brown dust.

Alexa rose, set the journal down well away from the glass of lemonade in case one of the dogs knocked it over, and strolled across the front yard to the gate.

She stood there as Stuart puttered up the dirt road. It was shocking to see the guy drive so slow. Was he still in pain? Maybe she shouldn't have invited him up here. Maybe he would be better resting back at home. As the car drew closer, the dogs all came rushing down, barking their heads off.

"Cool it!" she snapped.

They shut up, but kept a watchful eye.

She pushed the big metal gate open, its creaking reminding her that she needed to go to the ranch's machine shop and find some grease. Stuart stopped halfway inside the gate and rolled down the window. The dogs started barking again.

"Good to see you," he said with a grin. "I felt sure I'd get lost. Do you know you live next to a ghost town?"

"Bumble Bee isn't quite a ghost town. It gets RV folks in the winter. How are you feeling?"

"Fine. Why do you ask? I told you on the phone."

"I've been watching you for the last mile. You couldn't have been going more than twenty, and I've never seen you drive the speed limit."

Her partner's eyes went wide. "Driving a street vehicle on a dirt road? You crazy? Now if you gave me a Hummer, that would be a different story. I didn't want to get a flat and die of thirst out here."

Alexa laughed. "Come on in. The dogs won't bite."

Stuart's car crept along until he found a spot between Dad's and Wayne's pickups. He got out and pet the nearest dog, which started wagging its tail furiously.

"So you feel all right?" Alexa asked after she closed the gate and strolled up to him.

"Oh, yeah. Annette's got some unguent she makes herself. Old Mexican recipe. Not cream, not salve, but unguent. Ah, *unguent*. Rolls off the tongue, doesn't it? Un-gu-ent."

Alexa frowned. "You're not going to talk about Annette all weekend, are you?"

Stuart got a distant look in his eye, then seemed to snap out of it. "Uh, no. Probably won't talk *with* her either. She's got some big case. Working through the whole weekend. She's as much of a workaholic as you are."

"You're not exactly lazy yourself. Pop the trunk and I'll get your bags."

"I can get them."

"I'll get them. Then I'll get you a beer."

Alexa's father tromped out of the house, his eyes narrowing a little.

"You that Fed my daughter invited?"

"Yessir."

"Aren't you a little short to be a lawman?"

Stuart paused, obviously unsure what to say, so he deflected the question. "My commander always said I should have gone into the tank corps."

"Commander? You served?"

"Two tours of duty in Iraq."

"Four years in that hellhole, you get back in one piece, only to get shot by a girl? Damn, boy. Let me get you a beer and man you up."

He disappeared inside. Alexa let out a breath of relief. The way Dad's tone had changed from mocking challenge to gruff ribbing showed Stuart had passed muster. The old man hated Feds, but he respected the troops, so it had balanced out.

"He's just like you described him," Stuart said, open the trunk of his car. Alexa grabbed the bags before he could.

"He's all right." *Sort of.*

She led him into the house and one of the guest rooms. "You're right next to Stacy's room. The walls are thin so don't have any explicit conversations with your new girlfriend."

"Oh, she's not much of a talker. Takes nice selfies, though."

"Too much information. Let's go to the back porch. The others should be back there. Just a warning, my sister-in-law is here."

"The reporter?"

"Yeah."

Stuart's face hardened, although he tried to hide it. If Melanie hadn't been family, she was sure Stuart would have a few choice words to say about her.

So did Alexa, as a matter of fact.

And they almost came rushing out when she walked to the back porch and saw what Melanie was doing.

The reporter had been riding with Stacy and Malcolm. They were just dismounting in front of the barn, Melanie fumbling her way off the saddle and nearly falling despite having been married to a rancher for three years. Malcom took her reins to help her while Stacy led her own horse into the stable.

Alexa seethed. While there technically wasn't anything wrong with her sister-in-law going for a ride with one of Alexa's brothers, Alexa wanted to keep the nosy reporter as far away from Stacy as possible.

Plus she hadn't thought to warn the girl not to talk too much to Melanie. It never occurred to Alexa the city girl would go riding with them.

She's up to something.

Melanie wiped her hands on her jeans and headed for the house, leaving Malcolm to lead her horse into the barn.

When she caught sight of them, her face lit up with a smile, the same smile she used for the TV cameras. "Hi Alexa. Oh, isn't this your partner?"

"Yes. My name's Stuart," he said.

"I hope you're feeling better. How's the gunshot wound?"

Stuart put on an innocent face. "What gunshot wound?"

For a moment, Melanie looked confused. That confusion quickly turned into annoyance.

She put on her fake smile back on and turned to Alexa. “Well, I better go have a shower. I have to get back to Phoenix tonight. Early start tomorrow. Horses may look pretty, but they sure do smell!”

She walked into the house.

Alexa turned to Stuart. “Could you give me a minute?”

“Sure. I’ll go check out the barn.” He put on a bad John Wayne accent. “Maybe rustle up some dogies.”

“Do you even know what you’re saying?”

“Not really, no.”

Stuart headed for the barn. Alexa went inside.

She found Melanie at the sink washing her hands.

“I thought you were going to take a shower,” Alexa said, standing at the door.

“I need to wash my hands first. You can’t expect me to touch my towel or clean clothes with that animal stink on me, do you?”

Why did you marry a rancher?

Alexa didn’t ask that. She had a more important question to ask.

“What were you talking to Stacy about?”

“Oh, she did most of the talking. She was chattering on and on about horses. She likes taking care of yours. Smith and Wesson. Love the names. That’s a great detail. So charitable of you to take in a disadvantaged child. Action News does a Christmas charity drive every year. Toys for Tots. So rewarding. Wayne says her parents are drunks?”

“Don’t say that in front of her. It would upset her.”

“Of course not,” Melanie gave a little laugh.

“So what else did you talk about?”

Melanie didn’t look at her, merely gave a little shrug.

“Melanie?”

The reporter dried her hands on one of the towels “Oh, nothing! You can’t expect me to pay attention to everything some little trailer park girl says.”

Alexa’s hands balled into fists.

“You do know that it’s illegal for you to interview a minor without her parents’ consent, don’t you?”

Melanie gave another of her fake little laughs. Alexa had learned long ago that it was the reporter’s way of covering up nervousness.

“Who said anything about an interview?”

"You want to find out more about my work for some story you're cooking up. You're always badgering me for an interview and I always say no. So you want to get around that by—"

"All I did was talk to a kid who was already talking to me. Relax, Alexa. And why shouldn't someone write about you? You caught Drake Logan. And a few weeks later you caught another serial killer. You're a hero. Marshal Powers's wife certainly thinks so. Stacy told me how she came over and gave you—"

"You leave Robert out of this."

Melanie raised her hand in a placating gesture her face going serious. "You're grieving. I know. I'm sorry. I'm just saying that a bit of publicity would do you some good. You know how tense things are between the public and law enforcement right now. You're the perfect poster girl. You're smart and you have that down-home vibe people can resonate with. I—"

"I don't want to be written about, and I don't want you talking with Stacy."

"Don't worry. It was only a suggestion. All I'm asking is that you think about it. You can't keep your name out of the news entirely, not with the high-profile cases you've been getting. National news twice in two months!"

"I'm only doing my job."

"Doing a hell of a job!" Melanie gave her a punch on the shoulder that was meant to be chummy and only came off more fake than her smiles. "So think about it. A profile would do you good. Now I really need to take a shower. I have to wash my hair too, and it takes ages to dry."

Melanie moved as if to close the door. Alexa left, seething.

For she knew what Melanie was really after. Being Alexa's sister-in-law, she wanted to ride Alexa's fame to take a step up in her career. A "family interview" would be a coup, her ticket to a bigger TV market, like L.A. or New York City like she was always talking about.

And with that much of an incentive, Alexa knew, Melanie would get her interview one way or another.

CHAPTER THIRTY ONE

It had grown late. Stacy had crashed hours before, worn out by hours of riding and chores. Dad, as usual, had gone to sleep early. Wayne had gone to bed shortly afterwards. Both rose before the sun to start the daily round of ranch work. Malcolm was in his room, meditating or reading one of those spirituality books he obsessed over.

That left only Alexa and Stuart sitting on the back porch. They had switched off the lights to better see the brilliant canopy of stars and not to be bothered by bugs.

They sat in silence for a bit, listening to the distant forlorn howl of a coyote. Stuart seemed much more relaxed than she had ever seen him, although that might be as much due to the several beers he'd downed that afternoon and evening as any effect of the quiet countryside.

Stuart glanced at her, looked back out at the desert, then back at her.

"Can I ask you something?" he asked.

Alexa shrugged. "Sure."

"Why did you go into law enforcement?"

Because a ranch hand I had a crush on tried to rape me when I was sixteen. I broke his teeth with a horseshoe.

"I guess I always had a strong sense of justice."

"Being raised by someone like your dad I'm not surprised. He's a real law and order type."

"What about you?" Alexa asked.

"Well, after Iraq I came home and got a job at a sports center run by the city. Teaching middle-aged guys to use a climbing wall and obstacle course, stuff like that. Boring as hell. You can't hunt terrorists for four years and go into a job like that. A lot of guys go nuts when they try. Turn to drugs. Turn to booze." Stuart raised his beer with a guilty chuckle. "Or become mercenaries. I was offered a job as a merc. No way. So I looked for something interesting. Exciting. But smart too. Not just a regular cop. And I ended up trying out for the FBI."

Alexa nudged him. She was slightly tipsy too. "You got more excitement than you bargained for."

“I sure did. But really, after Iraq, even this job feels like a vacation. No sand flies. No car bombs. Well, the occasional house bomb. Hopefully that won’t be a regular threat. Plus I get to go home to a nice clean bed in a nice clean apartment where no one is sending rockets at it and I’m not sleeping next to dozens of guys all farting from the MREs.”

“Sounds like bliss.”

“Well, it’s good enough.”

The conversation lulled back into silence. For several minutes they stared out at the desert. A satellite, visible as a little white dot, rode a silent path across the sky.

“That’s not why I joined up,” Stuart mumbled.

“What was that?” He had spoken so quickly and softly Alexa wasn’t sure she had heard him correctly.

Stuart took a deep breath and said, “Iraq. That’s not why I joined up.”

Alexa turned to him. “So why did you?”

Stuart made a face. He glanced at her and then looked back out at the desert. The moment stretched out, and Alexa was beginning to think he wouldn’t answer when he said, “When I was sixteen, I had a girlfriend. Typical high school romance, but pretty serious. First love and all that.” He smiled, but the memory did not seem happy to him. “We dated for a year and a half, which is like forever when you’re that age. We both got pretty physical, as you can imagine, but we never went all the way. There was this old shed out in the woods where teens would go to make out. We went there a lot. Fool around, snuggle. But her pants stayed on. She said she wasn’t ready. I’ll be honest, that frustrated the hell out of me, but thanks to what I felt about her, and a whole lot of cold showers, I managed to be a gentleman.”

“Good for you.”

Stuart continued like he hadn’t heard. “Shortly after her sixteenth birthday, she told me she was ready. She said to meet her at that shed on Friday night. Man, I was over the moon. So happy. I asked if she was sure and she gave me a big kiss right there in the hallway of our high school and said she had been ready for a while but just wanted to think it through.

“So that night I drove to the woods where that shed was. I saw her car already parked there. It was a middle-of-nowhere place, so we felt safe. The only other people we ever saw were other teenaged couples coming for the same thing, and this time I didn't see any cars.

"I went down this dark little path that led to the shed. I had my flashlight with me, which I turned on once I was well out of sight of the road. I was surprised I didn't see my girlfriend's light. I was thinking she was going to jump out and try and scare me or something. She always played pranks like that."

Stuart laughed a little, but there was no heart in it. He went on.

"I got to the shed. She wasn't there. The only thing I saw was her torn shirt. The one I liked best. She had worn it specially for me. It was lying in front of the shed, covered in blood."

Alexa's breath caught. Stuart, as if sleepwalking, tonelessly continued.

"I called out to her. Ran around the woods like crazy for a while. God, I could have disappeared too if the guy had stuck around, but I saw no one. No other clues. Then I ran back to my car and drove like crazy back to town. Got the cops."

A tremor ran through Stuart's body. "They suspected me, of course. Questioned me. I don't think they ever really thought I was the prime suspect, though. And they sampled the blood on the shirt. There were two blood types, neither of them mine. One was my girlfriend's blood and the other was someone else's. She fought. Fought for her life. And if I had arrived a few minutes earlier I might have saved her."

Stuart hung his head.

"It's not your fault. You would have probably been killed too," Alexa told him.

"Everyone always says that," Stuart grumbled. "Even her parents said that. And it's true. Good luck actually feeling that, though. They never found who did it. Never found … her body either. Cold case. I looked it up after I joined the FBI, thinking I might find something the police in my hometown had missed. Nothing. There was so little evidence, and that was all so long ago. Whoever did it, got away with it. I don't want other people to get away with the same."

Alexa looked at her partner for a long time. He was a dim shape in the darkness, head hung low.

"I'd like to help you find him," she said, surprising herself with how much she meant it.

He looked at her with haunted eyes, slowly coming back from wherever he was.

He offered a weak smile at the corner of his mouth.

"That means a lot to me," he said. "More than you'll ever know."

He sighed.

"I'm not ready," he said. "Not now."

She nodded, understanding all too well.

"But when I am, you're the person I want at my side," he added, after a long pause.

He turned and offered her a genuine smile this time, and extended a hand.

"Partner," he added.

She shook it, firm and solid. Determined. Like her.

They let go, and each turned out to stare into the darkness of the desert. They sat in silence for a long while, until the sounds of night engulfed them, and Alexa felt the word ring within her.

Partner.

Yes.

For the first time in a long while, something sounded right.

NOW AVAILABLE!

<u>THE KILLING HOUR</u>
(An Alexa Chase Suspense Thriller—Book 3)

THE KILLING HOUR (An Alexa Chase Suspense Thriller—Book 3) is book #3 in a new series by mystery and suspense author Kate Bold, which begins with THE KILLING GAME (Book #1).

Alexa Chase, 34, a brilliant profiler in the FBI's Behavioral Analysis Unit, was too good at her job. Haunted by all the serial killers she caught, she left a stunning career behind to join the U.S. Marshals. As a Deputy Marshal, Alexa—fit, and as tough as she is brilliant—could immerse herself in a simple career of hunting down fugitives and bringing them to justice.

But with her recent work a big success, the FBI and the Marshals have decided to make their joint-task force permanent. Alexa, reeling from her own traumatic past and her PTSD of hunting serial killers, has no choice: she will now have to work with an FBI partner she dislikes and hunt down serial killers whose jurisdiction intertwines with that of the U.S. Marshals. Alexa finds herself forced to confront the thing she dreads the most—entering a killer's mind.

An infamous killer dramatically escapes death row, and Alexa's joint task force is immediately put on the case. A high profile case with national media attention, Alexa isn't the only one who's called in—and between the clashes of ego with other state and federal powers, she knows the killer is only getting further away.

What appears to be a straightforward manhunt, though, quickly evolves into something more complex, as more bodies turn up dead, and as the killer inexplicably eludes everyone.

And when a shocking twist occurs that Alexa never saw coming, she realizes this case is far more complex—and disturbing—than she could have ever imagined.

With the killer outsmarting everyone, Alexa is the only one with a mind brilliant enough to stop him, the only one standing between him and his next kill. But, weighed down by the pressure of her own traumatic past, can Alexa hold it together long enough to enter the darkest canals of his mind—and come out whole?

A page-turning and harrowing crime thriller featuring a brilliant and tortured Deputy Marshal, the ALEXA CHASE series is a riveting mystery, packed with non-stop action, suspense, twists and turns, revelations, and driven by a breakneck pace that will keep you flipping pages late into the night.

Future books in the series will be available soon.

Kate Bold

Debut author Kate Bold is author of the ALEXA CHASE SUSPENSE THRILLER series, comprising six books (and counting); and of the ASHLEY HOPE SUSPENSE THRILLER series, comprising three books (and counting).

An avid reader and lifelong fan of the mystery and thriller genres, Kate loves to hear from you, so please feel free to visit www.kateboldauthor.com to learn more and stay in touch.

BOOKS BY KATE BOLD

ALEXA CHASE SUSPENSE THRILLER
THE KILLING GAME (Book #1)
THE KILLING TIDE (Book #2)
THE KILLING HOUR (Book #3)
THE KILLING POINT (Book #4)
THE KILLING FOG (Book #5)
THE KILLING PLACE (Book #6)

ASHLEY HOPE SUSPENSE THRILLER
LET ME GO (Book #1)
LET ME OUT (Book #2)
LET ME LIVE (Book #3)